Based on a True Story

BASED
on a
TRUE
STORY

three novellas by
Hesh Kestin

**DZANC
BOOKS**

DZANC
BOOKS

1334 Woodbourne Street
Westland, MI 48186

www.dzancbooks.org

The Merchant of Mombasa first appeared in *Commentary Magazine*, August 2006.

Published 2008 by Dzanc Books
Book design by Steven Seighman

Cover photo: "The Couple, Vienna," 1935 by Trude Fleischmann, 14"x10 1/2" Vintage gelatin silver print from the Richard and Ellen Sandor Family Collection

06 07 08 09 10 11 5 4 3 2 1
First edition September 2008

ISBN: 0-9793123-5-3
ISBN-13: 978-0-9793123-5-9

Printed in the United States of America

Contents

For Leigh,
ever my love,
whose ardor and patience,
kindness and courage
have gotten us through a lifetime
of adventure, danger, hardship and
−that most perilous to romance—
the surreal minutiae of the day-to-day.
I would lie to suggest
words could not attempt
the depth and complexity
of what we share.
However inadequate,
they follow.

"Life knows us not and we do not know life - we don't even know our own thoughts. Half the words we use have no meaning whatever and of the other half each man understands each word after the fashion of his own folly and conceit. Faith is a myth, and beliefs shift like mists on the shore; thoughts vanish; words, once pronounced, die; and the memory of yesterday is as shadowy as the hope of tomorrow."

—Joseph Conrad, in a private letter

"Fiction . . . demands from the writer a spirit of scrupulous abnegation. The only legitimate basis of creative work lies in the courageous recognition of all the irreconcilable antagonisms that make our life so enigmatic, so burdensome, so fascinating, so dangerous - so full of hope."

—Joseph Conrad, in a published essay

The Merchant
of Mombasa

In converting Jews to Christians, you raise the price of pork.
                                            —William Shakespeare

Between the Hindu crematorium and the infectious-diseases hospital, Sergeants Mess was partially hidden by a stand of coconut palms and a large sign that seemed to have been imported directly from Trafalgar Square:

LOOSE LIPS SINK SHIPS
AND WILL RESULT IN
SEVERE DISCIPLINARY ACTION.
By order: Braithwaite, CO,
East Africa Command (Kilindini).

Just beneath the sign was a smaller version in Swahili, which I had been cramming since first we got word of J Group's transfer from Bletchley Park, home of His Majesty's Inter-Branch Cipher Command. With the fall of Singapore, the beginning of attacks on Ceylon, and India in line to be the next target of a seemingly unstoppable Japanese onslaught, one hundred fifty naval vessels of the Eastern Fleet had left the East to find shelter in and around Mombasa under the command of Vice Admiral Sir Hoddings Lord Braithwaite CBE, one of a raft of aristocrats who had become, by dint of birth and the exigencies of war, senior officers in His Majesty's service.

Lord Braithwaite may have been a bit of a stickler for what we in the Royal Canadian Air Force, from which I was on loan, called EBBU—Every Button Buttoned Up!—but when he had steamed into Kilindini Harbour aboard his flagship, HMS Warspite, and felt for himself the tremendous wet heat of Mombasa, he did have the good sense to revise previous orders and permit tropical kit: sleeves rolled to a regulation one inch above the elbow, knee-length trousers, calf-height cotton stockings, and one pair of dark glasses—or clip-ons for those who already wore spectacles.

The joke in Kilindini was that any spies in the vicinity would hardly have broken a sweat to identify the boffins from Bletchley Park: we were the ones wearing the clip-ons. Aside from a Dutchman named van Oost, who was so athletic he climbed Mt. Kilimanjaro two weeks after we set up in Kenya—I quit a thousand feet from the summit: as in codebreaking, the last steps in mountain climbing are the most difficult—we tended to look precisely what we were. With the exception of our group CO, who was a career officer, our ranking major, who had been something or other in CID, and Bailey, a sergeant like myself who had been in one of those spectral prewar cipher agencies, most of us were a mixed bag of prematurely balding, ill-at-ease types, quite a few with rather bad skin. It was as if the entire teaching staff of an English public school had been redeployed to East Africa. As the single Canadian, I was arguably odd man out, except that—along with Jenny Singleton and Amanda Hobbes, our company clerks—I could hardly claim the privilege.

The sudden appearance of women caused two problems, one immediate: as we clambered down the gangway of AMC *Alaunia*, wolf-whistles, accompanied by certain clearly understood gestures, could be heard from the deck of HMS *Royal Sovereign* docked alongside. Neither Singleton nor Hobbes seemed to know how to react; both were on the plain side, and this may have been the first time they were exposed to the undifferentiated lust of massed males. Perhaps less homely, I had been through it before.

The second problem was housing, which eventually solved the first.

It appeared no one had given the slightest thought to where to billet a collection of mathematicians. Tents were out of the question: although our brains were fit, many of us were past service age or otherwise frail. Our commanding officer, Paymaster Col. Moseley, who knew his way around a regiment, immediately paid a visit to HQ, where it was determined we should put up at a small hotel, the Lotus, and the next week move both our working and sleeping quarters to Allidina Visram School, an Indian boys' academy about a mile up the coast.

There remained the problem of security, both because of the presence of women—aside from a contingent of nurses, East Africa Command was almost entirely male—and because of our work. Though Bletchley Park, where we had undergone training, was sealed tighter than Downing Street, our quarters in Mombasa were wide open. In the end a detachment of the King's African Rifles was dispatched, the result of which was not so much to keep others out as to lock us in. Our days in the duty room were dedicated to monitoring Japanese wireless transmissions in the Indian Ocean, our nights spent mostly in a curry-scented prison where all the beds were three-quarter size and all the bathrooms held rather low-hung urinals, both something of a hazard for the taller men.

This was the least of it. Our duty room was full of flying creatures, from gnats and mosquitoes to a dependency of bats that lived in the rafters and preyed on a madrassa of praying mantises, each as long as a hand. For variety, the occasional snake slithered in to escape the heat, and a troupe of aggressive spider monkeys infested the grounds outside. Boredom was endemic. We quickly burned through most of the reading matter in the school library—there is only so much one can do with *The Hardy Boys' Missing Chums* and *Hopalong Cassidy's Rustler Round-Up*. With most of our working hours spent listening through earphones to wireless broadcasts, few of us had much patience for tuning in to the rare bit of music that reached us, weather permitting, from Nairobi. The work was demanding, often exciting when we made a breakthrough, but our leisure hours were no fun at all.

That is why when I received word to report to Vice Admiral Lord Braithwaite's residence the next day for high tea, I was as much delighted as I was terrified: both my uniforms were a sight. Singleton generously lent me her new skirt, and Hobbes did what she could with my hair, which had not been cut for a month and hung about my ears like a shapeless dirty-blonde mop. It simply was not made to stand up to the tropical heat, so heavy with humidity we often found it necessary to change our undies twice a day.

What was this high-tea business about? Neither my immediate superior, Lt. Fahnstock, nor our commanding officer, Col. Moseley, had a clue—or so they pretended.

II

Compared with our billet at the Indian boys' school, and the functional squalor of Sergeants Mess, to say nothing of the inadequately ventilated room we worked in eleven hours each day—one of our crew, Lammings, who had grown up in East London, likened it to a sweatshop, with mathematicians in lieu of Cockney sewing-machine operators—anything decent for tea would have been a godsend. Lord Braithwaite's official residence was more than decent. It was spectacular, a breathtaking white-marble cross between a stately home and a tea pavilion.

Apparently that is what it had been: the stately home of a principal tea grower, an Indian of some sort who had volunteered its use to His Majesty's Forces. After innumerable entry halls and foyers, each leading into the next like a series of Chinese boxes, I was escorted through a set of double doors that opened to reveal the stage-set drama of a veranda looking out over Kilindini Harbour, a table set for three, and two very different gentlemen standing by the alabaster balustrade and conversing so closely they might have been hatching a plot.

The adjutant who had taken me this far, quite dashing in that vacant way of the British landed gentry, turned silently on his heel just as we passed through the carved teak doors, and disappeared.

Lord Braithwaite was a massive figure in khaki whose gray mustache covered a good quarter of his pink face. The other gentleman seemed by comparison even frailer than he actually was. Balding, and wearing the kind of pince-nez that university dons liked to affect so that they might stare over them and dress you down for some horrid academic fault, he was attired in seriously out-of-date civilian clothes, including a cravat, something rarely seen in the steam room that was Mombasa. As though a bell had rung, both looked up abruptly.

"And you are, eh, sergeant, is it?"

I snapped a salute and held it. "Ferrin, sir. Sergeant, Royal Canadian Air Force, late of Bletchley Park, seconded to His Majesty's Navy, Kilindini. Sir!"

"Very good, Ferkin," Braithwaite said, smiling graciously under the broad whiskers that plumed out over his yellow, rather crooked teeth. He returned my sharp salute with something like a wave; he seemed almost to be scratching his head. Behind him the sun descended toward the horizon and mainland Kenya—the residence was situated on a spit of land jutting west into the harbor like a thumb surrounded on three sides by water. In the gardens sloping to the sea, its bright blue-green now tinged with gold, Royal Marine sentries in full dress paced like clockwork figurines. On either side, guard towers framed the view. "Needn't be so all-fired military, must we? Come and have a drink, sergeant. And do say hello to Mr. Albright. What are you these days, Cyril? Political adviser, what? Africa walla, that kind of thing."

"Political adviser, sir, if you wish," Albright said. Next to Braithwaite's energetic beefiness, he looked the very image of academic inutility, his suit, drab brown or olive or gray, hanging on him like a shroud. "So nice to meet you, sergeant. Canadian, you say." It was not a question. "Good people, the Canadians. The Frenchies amongst you can be a bit difficult, though. You're not . . .?"

"No, sir," I said. "From Alberta, really. Very few French there."

"I'm told you're something of an *mswahili*, is that true, sergeant?"

"Trying to learn it, sir. Out of a book. I've been practicing on the streets."

"Siku hiyo alikuja afisa mmoja Mzungu."

"I'm sorry, Mr. Albright. I don't—"

"On that day a European officer came."

"I meant to say—I did more-or-less understand the phrase—but wouldn't it be *sajini*, sir? I'm not an officer."

"Do they drink champagne at high tea in Alberta, Ferkin?" the vice admiral asked. He held out a flute already filled—I don't think I had seen a glass so delicate in my life. "Do relax, sergeant. Come and have a drink, a bit of smoked salmon. You do eat smoked salmon, don't you?"—he did not wait for a reply—"or there's some of this goose-liver paste. With the Jerries in France, a bit hard to come by these days."

"Unakula nyama ya nguruwe?" Albright asked.

"No, sir." I said. "I don't eat pork. But goose is fine." Fine? After the unidentifiable meat of Sergeants Mess, it was paradise.

"That you are, in fact, of a certain persuasion—*Myahudi?*"

"I am, sir. But I don't quite understand—"

"The vice admiral thought you might not be comfortable with victuals that would place you in a sticky spot."

"What do your people do?" Braithwaite said. "If you don't mind my asking, Ferkin."

Now I was thoroughly confused. Was he talking of my people, or *my people*? Never mind. I was to answer. "My father is a rancher, sir. Mum teaches. Mathematics, sir."

"Brothers, sisters?"

"No sisters, sir. One brother. RCAF. Missing over Burma, sir."

9

"Very sorry to hear," Braithwaite said, clearly not. "Know something of horses, do you?"

"I'm sorry, sir?"

"Horses," Albright jumped in, seeking to clarify by translating into a language I barely understood. "You know, *farasi*."

"I grew up on a horse." Consciously I omitted the sir. Instead I turned to the vice admiral, himself turned away to peer out over the bay. The lights of Mombasa were just coming on—how different from England, where under threat of German air raids the night brought only darkness and fear. "Vice Admiral Braithwaite, sir," I said to his back. "I'm a bit confused. I'm RCAF on loan to His Majesty's Navy for the purpose of assisting in code-breaking operations under supervision of Bletchley Park. I am a mathematician. I have no idea what my religion and, and . . .horses have to do with my work. Should I be offended, sir?"

That was the closest I could get to a complaint. There were two other Jews in our group—why was I being singled out? Was it because I was Canadian? That made no sense. And the horse business . . .I watched Braithwaite turn slowly to face me, his lips pursed beneath his mustache as though in consideration of some great question of naval strategy upon whose outcome hung the fate of the Empire.

"Sergeant, effective immediately, I am promoting you flight lieutenant. As such, you are hereby attached indirectly to my staff. You will be my principal adviser on matters equine and Judaic. As of tomorrow morning, I want you to begin work on securing for me a number of horses."

"I'm a code-breaker, sir."

"Code-breaker, horse-breaker, all the same, what. As I say, you will help me to secure at least two horses. If possible, seven."

I could not stop myself. "Jewish horses, sir?"

Albright looked down at me over his pince-nez and tapped the champagne flute in his hand as though it were a school bell. "Not Jewish horses, Ferrin," he said with a mixture of kindness and exasperation. "Horses from a Jew."

This left me no more enlightened. "Sir, I'm afraid I—"

"Afraid?" Braithwaite snorted, at once avuncular and all-powerful, as though he had adopted an orphan whom he would protect, but only so long as she behaved. "I don't know about you, Ferkin, but I do get a bit peckish at this hour, and would so like to eat. Mr. Albright hardly ever appears hungry, expected from a vegetarian—I believe they teach them that at Oxford, from which he's come to educate me on the native scene—but I'll wager *you* could do with a change from Sergeants Mess."

"Yes, sir. I think so, sir."

"So there's nothing to be of afraid of, really, is there? Now, come and sit, and we'll tell you all about it." He smiled more deeply as I stepped toward the table set with silver and china and Irish linen, all marked with the admiral's crest. "Jewish horses. Very good, wouldn't you say, Cyril? Imagine the circumcision. Jewish horses, indeed."

III

The owner of said Jewish horses, and of much of Mombasa, was one A.S. Talal, also proprietor of Talal General Stores, the Selfridges of Kenya, with large branches here and in Nairobi and smaller outlets in Kisumu and Nakura; Talal

Transport, the principal bus company—one traveled to Nairobi by rail, but TT was the virtual monopoly within the main towns; and Talal Brewers, producers of Green Tiger Lager, Black Circle Stout, and a line of non-alcoholic beverages including, under license from Schweppes, bottled waters, fruit juices, and an intensely sweet potion called Ken-Kola that was popular with His Majesty's Forces because it could be readily fermented. Startled newcomers to Mombasa often took cover from the sound of Ken-Kola bottles exploding in the night.

Talal was clearly profiting from the military invasion. Officers smoked his Kilimanjaro-brand cigarettes—packaged to look like Players—while other ranks tended to roll their own from the locally grown Royal Virginia Estates Blend, also Talal's. When uniforms wore out (women's excepted—I had mine made up by a local dressmaker) as they did with amazing rapidity in the moist climate, off-the-peg replacements were available from cloth woven by Talal Mills and sewn by Talal Tailors Ltd. The ferries that moved in the harbor were Talal's, the plantations of coconut in the lowlands and, of conspicuous value, tea in the highlands were Talal's, and—I was given to understand—the same individual had at one time played a significant role in the business of betting, which was the nonwhites' chief hobby, followed closely by adultery and alcohol. (Among the European residents the order of preference was said to be reversed.)

If I had thought this louche background made A.S. Talal seem vaguely romantic, like an American gangster who had, as they said in Edward G. Robinson movies, gone legit, I could not have been farther off-base. Like most successful Indians in Africa, A.S. Talal was hard-headed and narrowly focused. He may also have been the most off-putting man I had ever met.

This was not because he had mangled features or missing limbs. For an Indian, his skin was lighter than most, his features almost European—though his nose was quite large and as hooked as any in a Nazi propaganda poster—and his manner of dress and personal hygiene more than acceptable. It was his ego, which could have swallowed up Lord Braithwaite's and Cyril Albright's together. What I found repellent was not his appearance but his attitude.

"A flight lieutenant?" he said to me on first sight, pronouncing it the way the Brits did, *left-tenant.* "I should have thought wing commander at least. Young lady, would you mind terribly going back to your superiors and coming back a colonel, or a general? We've got four generals in Mombasa these days. Surely Braithwaite can spare just one?"

I wasn't sure how to take this, or if the taut glare on his smooth, unlined face was its natural condition. "I'm certain that can be arranged, Mr. Talal," I said, with the intention of not backing off. "But you wouldn't want the admiral to raise someone in rank merely to impress you. I had heard you were shrewder than that."

Now he looked at me in a different way. His jaw relaxed a bit, and behind his thick frameless lenses that were darkened into some sort of deep rose I could just make out a light, a glint perhaps.

"What is your mission, flight lieutenant?"

"It was explained to me as liaison, sir."

"You can drop the 'sir,' young lady."

"You may drop the 'young lady,' sir."

He smiled. "And if I drop her, will she break?"

We were in his office, a room about three times the size of the duty room at Allidina Visram School, and rather more tidy. For one thing, no flies or bats. Talal's desk was a large Indo-Biedermeier affair of what appeared to be ebony, rather intricately and deeply carved on the legs—it might have started out in life as a dining table—with brass repoussé on the surface protected by glass. From my angle, in the single chair opposite, purposely designed to be somewhat lower than his, the relief appeared to be a tableau of ganeshas, the elephant-headed gods of success, figures as complex and detailed as those in the ceiling of the Sistine Chapel. But in the Vatican one looked up in order to feel the grandeur of the heavenly host and the insignificance of man. Here Talal looked down, the gods encased in glass at his fingertips.

"I am hardly that fragile, Mr. Talal."

"I expect not, if Braithwaite sent you."

A long moment ensued. Talal's large table before me, I decided to lay my cards, such as they were, upon it. "The vice admiral has heard you are in possession of something he desires."

"Mombasa?"

"The vice admiral already has that."

"Only superficially," Talal said. "It's a tricky place."

"Mombasa is under military rule, sir."

"My dear, for a thousand years Mombasa has been under military rule—of the Galla, the Zimba, the Swahili, the Omani many times, the Dutch, the Turks, the Portuguese any number of times, the Swahili yet again, and now the British. But Mombasa does not succumb. To govern here is one thing, to rule another."

"Nevertheless, Mr. Talal—"

"Would you like to see my stables now, flight lieutenant, or would you prefer to discuss these matters in the abstract?"

He must have seen the surprise I quickly covered with a smile. How did he know? "If you wish, sir."

"Please do call me Abraham."

It would be a week before I could bring myself to that. "I would be honored to see what it would please you to show, Mr. Talal."

He snorted, then carefully removed his glasses and, with a handkerchief so white it glowed, slowly and methodically cleaned the lenses. His eyes were large, and of a shade that made the brilliant azure of the harbor seem muddled and gray. I had never seen an Indian with blue eyes before and must have stared. He replaced the spectacles and stood.

"Ferrin," he said. "Ferrin. What sort of name is that?"

"Canadian, sir."

"Come now, flight lieutenant. There is no such thing as a Canadian name. Beyond the poor Eskimos and Aleuts, Red Indians and so on, all Canadians are immigrants. What sort of Canadian are you?"

"My family emigrated from Russia before the turn of the century."

"Orthodox, then? Where the priests marry? Long beards? Those big black hats?" He was toying with me.

"Jewish Canadian," I said.

He raised his head, as though to look at me from another angle. "Ahhhh . . ." He stretched out the sound until it seemed to be less a recognition than a sigh. "Send a Jew to deal with a Jew. Very clever man, your Braithwaite. But hardly subtle. Not subtle at all."

As I accompanied Talal, who was a bit shorter than I—his trunk was somewhat too long for his legs—out of the office and down steps leading to grounds as manicured as my nails had been in another life, I realized finally that what was so off-putting about the man was also, to me at least, so attractive. He was smarter than those around him,

15

knew it, and wanted you to know it too, not so much to impress but to get this awkward bit of business out of the way. On the gravel path to his stables, I discovered I didn't care. Smart was what I liked. It had always been what I liked. If that had to be wrapped in ego, it was a small price. I found I rather liked Abraham Talal.

IV

After moving up so abruptly in rank I was no longer permitted to continue dining at Sergeants Mess, and missed it. No merit had attended my promotion to the dining room of the Imperial Hotel: I didn't belong.

The unease was general, but only at first. My former superior, Charlie Fahnstock, a rather stout and dour fellow who had grown up in Kenya before studying statistics at the London School of Economics—to His Majesty's Forces, statistics was close enough to mathematics— introduced me into my new setting. Like most of the Bletchley Park crew, I was protective of Charlie: he was hardly, as the code-breakers liked to rhyme, a "deft-tenant," and probably should not have been in the armed forces at all; he had no leadership abilities whatsoever. But he did speak Swahili—and he meant well.

"G-gentlemen," he said with the stammer that young men of good family affected in those days, "th-this is Ferrin. Newly c-c-atapulted from the sergeantry to the off-off-officerial c-class. Unlike y-yours truly, c-clearly a case of m-m-merit." Exhausted by his expedition into public speaking, he fell upon his seafood bisque as though he had not eaten for days.

After this, the others were quite welcoming. The prospect of sex might have had something to do with it: officers were discouraged from social intercourse with other ranks and, unlike in Nairobi, there were few unattached European women on the coast. After a few minutes, it was quite as though I had been an officer forever.

Certainly the African servants could not have known otherwise: our waiter trotted off to the kitchen for a replacement when he noticed I did not touch my soup. Though as a Jewish family in Alberta we had not been particularly rigid regarding the dietary laws, neither shellfish nor pork had ever appeared in our kitchen, and the very idea of eating them turned my stomach.

"Don't fancy the bisque, Ferrin?" The speaker was a terribly good-looking young squadron leader named Trent-Smith—he could not have been more than twenty-two.

"Allergic to shellfish, I'm afraid," I said, smiling.

"Damn shame," he said. "It's not the best thing about the local fodder, it's the only good thing. I haven't had a decent chop in months."

Had he been compelled to eat at Sergeants Mess, poor Trent-Smith might have felt better. I was not so blasé. Officers Mess at Kilindini was at the level of the prewar Savoy in London—I had dined there with my visiting parents when I was at Cambridge—or the Ritz-Carlton in Montreal, where my dear lost brother had once treated me to an expensive spread. One could get used to Officers Mess: real butter on the table, salad so crisp it crackled, starched linen, servants so well-trained one hardly finished one's plate before it was smoothly replaced with the next, and somehow or other no flies. Probably they were all at Sergeants Mess.

At the evening meal, just as I was seated, the brisk adjutant, who had shown me to the veranda only days before and abruptly vanished, now reappeared. "Vice Admiral Lord Braithwaite requests your presence at table," he said. "Lieutenant."

Every eye in the vast hall was upon me as I followed him, threading my way through the sea of ensigns and lieutenants, a lake of captains and majors, a puddle of colonels and commanders, and a sprinkling of brigadiers and rear admirals until, by windows overlooking the harbor— Braithwaite seemed to prefer a clear avenue of escape— I found myself at a table once again set for three. I saluted.

"Do sit, Ferkin," Braithwaite said. He had an enormous prawn in his right hand, with which he tossed off what passed for a salute. "Improvement on Sergeants Mess, what?"

"Yes, your lordship." He continued to work on the prawn. "*Shikamoo*, Mr. Albright." It was the way one greeted an elder—I had just learned this refinement. "Always good to see you."

Unlike the vice admiral's, his plate was untouched: on one side, three slices of tomato; on the other, a bed of lettuce. I had the feeling Albright rarely ate, like some reptile who waited patiently in ambush to swallow something bigger than himself. "*Marahaba*," he said, speaking as an elder. "*Hupendi samakigamba?* It is my understanding you don't care for shellfish." "We share that."

"At least Albright has a decent reason, Ferkin."

"Allergic, actually," the civilian said. "Animal protein. It makes me ill."

I nearly laughed: so my excuse actually made sense in the real world.

"You know, Ferkin," the vice admiral grunted cheerily, wiping his gray mustache with a linen napkin bearing his crest, "your religion has got you people into quite a mess, hasn't it?"

"My religion, sir?"

"*Chinjo la wayahudi.*"

"I don't know the first word, Mr. Albright."

"Massacre, *chinjo*. Plural, *machinjo*."

"Bloody foolishness, holding onto these rituals. Cuts you off from the mass of men. I daresay you people wouldn't be in the state you're in, Nahzees and all that, were it not for the fact you do keep yourselves apart."

"I was at school with a Jewish fellow," Albright said, as though mining the past. "Gold something."

An African servant came up just in the nick of time—I don't know where the conversation might have led—with a plate of curried chicken, green salad, and, for some reason, a little tent of six leaning gherkins. Clearly the plate had been put together especially for me.

"I've seen the horses, sir," I said brightly, not waiting to be asked—anything to get the vice admiral and his civilian flunky off their talk of crustaceans and Nahzees. Another moment and I might have said something. If Braithwaite wanted to send me back to Sergeants Mess—where no one ever noticed what I ate or did not eat or, if they did, had the courtesy not to comment—so much the better.

"You have?"

"Yes, sir. They're splendid."

"Splendid," Braithwaite said, his mustache once again surrounding a prawn. "Or merely unusual?"

I popped a gherkin into my mouth. The remaining five tumbled into a ragged pile on the plate. "Both, sir." I chewed on the gherkin—nothing had tasted so delicious since I'd left home—while Braithwaite gnawed on a fresh prawn with what I supposed was impatience.

Albright broke the silence. "Come, come, lieutenant, there's a war on. We haven't got ages."

"Very well," I said, once again avoiding direct response. Instead I turned physically to the vice admiral. "There are seven—two stallions, the rest mares. There may be more but that is all I saw. They are Marwari, sir. I suppose you know that."

Braithwaite picked up his glass, South African hock, the chilled green bottle shining in a silver ice bucket glistening with rivulets of sweat. He swallowed down a considerable amount. "Yes, Marwari. Tell me what I don't know."

It occurred to me to tell him that he did not know I felt closer to Abraham Talal than ever I could to his lordship, but I dared not. "Just over fifteen hands, the stallions, the mares about fourteen. As you are probably aware, the breed is distinguished for its long, pointed ears that taper gracefully and turn in toward each other as if in conversation. Looked at head-on, they form a lyre shape. From the side the head is long and aquiline, straight as this table, sir, with large flaring nostrils and gentle lips."

"Go on."

"They are a beautiful horse, sir. Straight back, strong vertical limbs. Extremely tough hooves. A farrier's nightmare—they run unshod. Mr. Talal was kind enough to explain—"

"Kind enough, my left foot," Braithwaite said suddenly, so loudly that officers several tables away looked up. "The man is keen on *selling* his livestock. Kind enough, indeed. He's playing at this damned . . .eastern game. Arabs, Jews, Indians—an infernal bad habit is all it is. Lieutenant, I am more than familiar with the Marwari strain, at least from books. There are, unfortunately, very few of them these days *outside* of books, what with the coming of motor transport and our policy of defanging the maharajas. Before the Great War you might find any odd Indian ruler with a small cavalry, 200-500 horses, sometimes a 1000. But there are precious few now. Frankly, I think the damned Indians *ate* them. Regardless, our Mr. Talal certainly has the only purebred Marwaris in Africa. For all I know, he has the only purebred Marwaris anywhere.

"Now stop looking at me with your mouth open, lieutenant, and help me save the last of this breed and bring them to England where they belong, and can be bred, and will be looked after, and get them out of the hands of your Mr. Talal. Mis-ter Ta-lal, oh yes. You know, for a farthing, I would simply seize the lot as military necessity, but those fops in the War Office would have my head, and Whitehall would be upset—present company excepted, Cyril—and there'd be hell to pay. Now go and buy me these ponies, like a good chap, Ferkin, and don't come back without them." He considered. "Splendid, eh? They're not splendid, lieutenant, they're priceless. Now go and get me a price."

V

Were Abraham Talal's horses for sale? In theory, everything Talal owned was for sale. He was, if nothing else, a merchant. But he had not become the principal merchant of Mombasa simply because he bought and sold—everyone on the coast did that, and had for centuries. His secret was the same kind of intelligence we in J Group were in the business of collecting. His methods may have been different, but he clearly spent a great deal of time and money staying informed.

Thus, only a month before the Bletchley Park crew's arrival in Mombasa, Talal had acquired the Lotus Hotel, which was to remain fully occupied by British personnel throughout the war; it was the only second-class hotel on the island with toilet facilities for each room. Whether it was how much to expand production at his cement works at Ndega, or how much to bid on military-construction contracts that would utilize the same cement, he made it his business to know. His dozens of managers—Hindus on the coast, Europeans of one sort or another in the uplands—reported to him regularly with a flood of information.

Making sense of it must have been a challenge, in perhaps the same way as we code-breakers faced a torrent of Japanese ciphers that remained meaningless without the all-important key. In our situation we were unable to ask further questions; Talal was not so limited. Against the Indian stereotype, he was generous in compensating his staff, who knew they were being spoiled and wished this to continue. Spread throughout the country, they were adept at laying their hands on the right information or the person who could get it. Politically, Talal was equally well-connected. It was said he was generous here as well. Certainly he seemed to have a direct line to HQ East Africa Command. Just as certainly, the vice admiral knew it.

This must have been galling to Braithwaite, who could not have been unaware that inviting A.S. Talal for dinner might have gone a long way toward smoothing the path for His Majesty's Forces on the coast. But vice admirals apparently did not deign to sup with merchants, Indian merchants especially, and Jews so much the less. Sending me out to deal with Abraham must therefore have seemed only proper to Lord Braithwaite.

But to Talal the indirect approach was something between annoyance and insult, not least because little that went on in the CO's vicinity remained unknown to him: after all, Braithwaite was ensconced in Talal's primary residence, which His Majesty's forces had more or less commandeered for the duration of the war. Of course the house came with Talal's servants, who must have been a principal conduit of intelligence, though it puzzled me that Talal was aware of matters somewhat too sophisticated for mere Shirazi domestics to pick up. Perhaps some of these servants were more clever than they let on.

We were riding on the beach at Jumba la Mtwana, having been ferried to the mainland from Talal's private dock in Mombasa, the horses apparently accustomed to this form of transportation. I was on a lovely piebald mare named Rajshree, my host on Mewar, a skewbald stallion with ears as long as my jodhpurs. I had told Abraham I had no riding clothes. That morning a superb set of boots, britches, and jersey, along with a black-velvet-covered helmet, was delivered to my quarters at the school—all my size, even my taste.

Rajshree was easy in the reins, responsive to the slightest signal, and loved to run on the packed sand, small waves spilling over and wetting her unshod hooves in what seemed to be adoration. I had not had such fun on horseback since riding at home on the ranch with David, of whom I had heard nothing since his plane had disappeared four months earlier. I can't say this was not on my mind as Rajshree swept over the sand in a curious gait halfway between a gallop and a canter, so smooth there was almost no vertical motion—Abraham was later to describe this to me as the *ravaal*, a movement unique to Marwaris—and I stuck to the high-canted cavalry saddle as though glued.

We dismounted at a grove of coconut palms, where servants were waiting with lunch.

"Abraham, you do live well," I said.

"I consider it compensation."

"Against?"

"Against the moment when I do not."

"I should think you would accept the inevitability."

"Oh, I do," he said. "My Hindu friends see things differently, but for me there is only this life."

"And for your Hindu wife?"

He was washing his hands in a copper bowl that had been set up on a bamboo tripod by the table, stopped quite sharply, then resumed. I had just gone through the same wash-up. A servant handed him a dry cloth. "Your intelligence is as good as mine," he said. "Lieutenant."

"I had to know."

He nodded as he cleaned salt spray from his roseate spectacles with the cloth. "Precisely. What is it you don't know that I can tell you?" He forced a smile. "Joan."

"I didn't mean to embarrass you."

"I am not embarrassed. Merely surprised."

"Surprised?"

"That you would care, one way or the other."

It was time for me to force a smile. "You can't think very highly of me, Abraham, if you think I wouldn't."

"Perhaps I was being hopeful," he said. "Would you like to eat, or are you too angry?"

"Never too angry to eat," I said. "And not really angry at all. Disappointed, perhaps."

"Disillusioned?"

"Canadians have no illusions."

"Because they have no dreams?"

"Because we have no past," I said. "We're all fresh,

new in the world. So we're perfectly happy with what we've got. Like children with a new toy. Or a new friend."

"I'd like to be your friend, Joan. May I be your friend?"

"If I may have some curry," I said, "I'll give it thought."

He snapped the fingers of his left hand. A servant brought a silver dish, and from it deftly placed a serving spoon of curried fish, delicately flavored with cardamom and turmeric, on my china plate. Early on, I was never served meat in Abraham's presence. Perhaps his intelligence agents had already told him to avoid anything that might contravene my sensitivities, but a diet heavy in fish was—I was to learn—only natural for him: my sensitivities were his as well. He himself never ate pork, never shellfish, and the lamb or beef that showed up for dinner Friday evenings, when I began staying the weekend, was miraculously kosher, sent packed in ice by a Jewish butcher in Nairobi on the overnight train that chugged into Mombasa every morning at 8 AM. The Lunatic Line, they called it, because of the hairpin turns that sent it hurtling down from the highlands. For Abraham Talal it must have been anything but. It allowed him the sanity of a Sabbath meal. "I do have a wife, Hindu, yes, and three children. Daughters. I will show you photos if you like. Very pretty girls, eight, ten, and twelve years of age. Charming girls. Good students. I expect they will be educated at university in England. Would you recommend Cambridge or Oxford?"

"I was at—"

"Cambridge," he said. "I know."

"What don't you know?"

"Whether Oxford or—"

"Cambridge for the sciences, I think. Are they scientific, your daughters?"

"Rather too early to tell, I'm afraid. Did you enjoy—"

"Cambridge?"

"Science, maths, that sort of thing?"

"Since I was a child," I said. "As I grew older, math specifically. Most girls don't tend that way, or aren't encouraged."

"I shall encourage my girls in that direction, if they wish," he said. "If you wish."

"My parents did, actually. Sent me off to McGill, and then I went up to Cambridge."

"You could be at Cambridge now."

"When the war came I volunteered for the Royal Canadian Air Force."

"You can say RCAF."

"RCAF. My brother had already joined up."

"It must be very difficult for you."

"You needn't say it like that. He's missing is all. Missing flyers come back all the time. He's an outdoorsman, tough as nails, and extremely adaptive. I wouldn't be surprised if he is walking out of Burma as we speak." Did I really believe this? It was what I told myself every night when my head hit the hard pillow at Allidina Visram School. If anyone could survive that kind of ordeal, it was David. But perhaps I told myself this because I was unsure I could survive my own ordeal if it were otherwise. "He rode a bicycle once from Calgary to Montreal to visit me. Took three months. twenty-two hundred miles." I was truly embarrassed now. There was no comparing this to bailing out over Burma and walking out alive, if he could walk. It was a foolish thing to say, a foolish, girlish, hero-worshippingly hopeful thing to say. My face flushed.

Abraham reached across the table and took my hands in his. They were surprisingly soft—not like a woman's but like a child's. For a moment I was ill at ease.

Mine were large and bony by comparison, the hands of a rancher's daughter. And then, as though in preparation for some fate I could not know but suspected, my hands relaxed in his as he began to speak.

"You will no doubt think badly of me," he said. "And if so, you must have all the facts. Better to know than to guess. Joan, I am a man who has made my choices and... I live with them. When I came out to Kenya in '29 I can't say I had nothing, but close. One-hundred-twenty pounds sterling, letters of introduction to persons in the Indian community in Nairobi and in Mombasa. My father had died the year before—"

"I'm sorry."

"That was thirteen years ago," he said gently. "And father was 81. We're long-lived, the Talals. He was a live-stock dealer in Rajasthan, as his father had been, and his. Horses, cattle, sheep, goats. Even chickens sometimes. Never pigs, of course. And camel. Many, many camel. And elephant. In father's time Rajasthan, the Rajput states then, was more or less cut off from the world. The maharajas retained their independence from the central government, an independence that would diminish over the years as the British, in their clever way, bought off the nobility. "Our specialty was the Marwari. We supplied the cavalry mounts for all of Rajasthan and the Northern Frontier, a desert country but a good business. When my father was a young man, the Maharaja of Jhaipur kept three thousand men under arms, most on horseback. These were the same cavalry, the same type of men, the same type of horse, that had turned back the Moghul invaders, man and horse leaving the field only victori-ous or dead. Our stud held hundreds of mares, dozens of stallions of the best type. Black and white, brown and white, silver, chestnut. All well-conformed to the Marwari standard, long ears meeting in an arch, aquiline nose, the large nostrils, the same body type you see here, thin coats like silk, big eyes, straight legs, unslanted shoulders, hooves like steel. You are seeing them now, but I am told today that in India there are few pure Marwari left.

"Joan, when this war is over, the British will find themselves with mountains of tanks, continents of warships, fields upon fields of decommissioned warplanes. They will be sold for scrap. No one needs armament when there is no war. So it was with the Marwari. The maharajas did not require horses beyond a few for ceremonies, and the British cavalry preferred larger animals, less hot-blooded, hunter-jumpers, fox-hunt horses, not racing horses, not war horses. They brought over Walers from Australia, capable of carrying heavier loads. Our Indian horsemen are lighter, and were lightly equipped. The Marwari are fast, meant for the desert—notice their legs are almost perpendicular to the ground, which makes them fast on sand, as you have seen. They can pull them out of soft earth more quickly than—am I boring you?"

I looked at him. "Never."

"It's not often I can talk of this."

"How often?" I asked.

"Never," he said.

"Then don't be shy."

A laugh exploded from his face, and he seemed as young and innocent as the hands that held mine. "I am not shy," he said. "I am . . .unaccustomed. It is not my habit to— what is it you North Americans say? I was a great reader of Jack London as a boy—'spill my gut'?" He seemed to relax now. The servants, ever hovering, had gone to groom the horses they had tethered, unsaddled, in the coconut grove, the only sounds their movement, an occasional whinny, and the gentle surf. "Joan, we had the patent, as you might say, on the Marwari horse. For two hundred years we Talals of Jhaipur sold only mares and geldings. The stallions remained ours. And then, suddenly, the way battleships and fighter planes and submarines will be worthless after this war, our treasure was worthless—there were no more wars. The maharajas having been pacified, their cavalry was merely an expense. The Marwari had become a thing of the past. I selected the best stock, the rest . . ."

"You needn't say it."

"And with them came here." His eyes wandered, as though to a past I could not share. "The Indian community in Kenya is a community of traders, merchants. Perhaps as an Indian and a Jew I may say I was as bred for this as the Marwari were bred for war. The people here welcomed me. They knew my family, my father, his father. Sikh, Jain, Hindu, Muslim, Christian, Jew—whatever it was that caused strife amongst us in India melted away here. There was enough for all. The Africans—even the Shirazi on the coast who have been traders for a thousand years—were no match. The whites rarely wished to dirty their hands. In time I became... what I am."

"And married."

"Perhaps I should have brought a Jewish wife from Calcutta, the custom of my family because we were the only Jews in Jhaipur, in all of Rajasthan. Or sought a Jewish bride from the European community in Nairobi. That way my daughters would be Jews, and I would not be the end of my line, like my horses. But in those days, even more than now, crossing the color barrier was not lightly done, and I did not feel I had to beg for anyone's hand. Soon enough, as young men do, I fell in love." He shrugged. "And that is the story of my life, Joan. Full of quirks, perhaps, but not unusual, not at base." He paused. A wave broke, the wind picked up. "Until now."

VI

That night I attended the weekly concert beneath the walls of Fort Jesus, the Portuguese outpost that had stood here since the 16th century. Attendance was hardly mandatory. The only ones constrained to listen were those within the walls: having kept its enemies out for four hundred years, Fort Jesus now kept them in. It had become a brig.

How quaint it must seem now, but during the war, with so little certain—London itself was under almost nightly air attack—it was oddly comforting to sit on blankets on the sandy ground while an augmented phonograph played Tommy Dorsey and Artie Shaw. The heat had broken, a steady breeze came from the dhow harbor, and the ever-present mosquitoes, which the Bletchley Park crew had designated the Kenyan national bird, must finally have succumbed to our home-brewed repellent of three parts diesel fuel, one part each lime juice and coconut oil. Sometimes it worked, sometimes not. The mix was volatile: Jenny and Mandy, our clerks, experimented with adding perfumes, but what started out as lavender might during the course of an evening distill itself into something akin to burning tires, and an innocent sandalwood, widely available in the Arab shops—it probably came from Persia as in ancient times, via Oman across the water—became pungently musky, strongly suggestive of the scent that blossoms with exercise, or fear, or intimacy.

Not that we girls needed scent to inspire interest. Hardly beauties, the clerks had the pick of every enlisted man in coastal East Africa, and since being promoted I had found myself in the same kind of high demand among my fellow officers—not so much a compliment as a bother. Now, while the Andrews Sisters swung out "Boogie Woogie Bugle Boy of Company B," another voice broke through. It was a rich baritone, full of that languid timbre cultivated by Englishmen of a certain background.

It was Trent-Smith, the young squadron leader at whose table I had dined the first day in Officers Mess. "Fancy Patti, Maxene and LaVerne, do you?" he said, sitting himself down next to me like a fresh wine glass inserted at an already crowded table. He had all but forced his way between myself and a bulky naval captain with a sharply etched David-Nivenesque mustache. "Just for the moment, old stick," he said, not waiting for permission, and turned back to me. "It's queer how we've colonized Africa only to have African music colonize us."

"The Andrews Sisters are white," I said.

"Their music isn't. Don't get me wrong. I do love jazz. But I hear they're drinking an awful lot of Coca-Cola in England these days."

"We Canadians are used to it," I said. "We're the 49th state."

"Rather do like the Yanks," he said. "Individually. Massed, they are a bit much. But we *are* flying their planes, dropping their bombs. Hard to dislike them for it. Not impossible, but hard. Bite the hand and all that."

The Americans had been in the war for three months by now, and even in East Africa we were beginning to feel their presence. Since January, we shared our results on the Japanese codes with Washington, and as we cracked one cipher after another it was in everyone's mind that the Americans would be able to do quite a lot more than the Royal Navy with the fruits of our labor. For one thing, they had submarines and were building more every day. My work on J8, the secondary code of the Japanese commercial fleet, especially the tankers, was coming along, but I felt I should be doing more; the other significant ciphers—J2, J3 and J6—had already been broken. But code-breaking is as much a function of time as anything else, and since my elevation to the officer corps I was frequently called away on liaison duties, a good deal of which, I admit, were of my own making.

If my job was to get close to Abraham Talal . . .very well then, I would do so. We dined together nightly, toured the Arab shops on Dika Street together, and went on long rides along the coast. On today's trek we had gone inland to visit the site of an abandoned city where, as if by pre-arrangement, Abraham was able to sift in the ruins and come up with a shard of porcelain. "Ming," he said. "These people were first-class merchants. You'll find Persian bits as well and, if we search long enough, Venetian coin. Hard to believe, but at one time this was a center of commerce." Whatever had compelled the inhabitants to flee—raids by Galla horsemen from the north, by Zimba cannibals from the inland forests, possibly a final attack by the Portuguese, perhaps lack of water—whatever the cause, there was now a finality about the place that was, even in the hot wet, chilling. Mombasa itself had been three-times destroyed and three-times rebuilt. Here the inhabitants had decamped never to return, leaving behind their pots, sticks of furniture, cloth, even pets: while our horses grazed nearby, Abraham casually pointed out the brittle skeleton of what could only have been a dog.

"Nothing lasts, does it?" he said. It was not a question, but a statement of fact.

I chose to hear it differently. "It can. Rather depends on will. Look at Mombasa."

"Yes," Abraham said, removing his roseate lenses so that I could see his eyes, somewhat bloodshot from the dust of the inland ride. "But Mombasa is only Mombasa. It's never been Rome or London or New York. It's lasted because no one ever demanded much of it. Nothing was ever created here. It's just trade. A lot of it, but just trade."

"*Are you there, Ferrin?*" It was Trent-Smith. "You seem miles away."

"Just caught up in the music," I lied.

He leaned close. "Do you think we could meet after the concert? I know a place."

For an Englishman Trent-Smith was refreshingly direct. Perhaps it was the war, or the American influence, or maybe he had simply discovered that it worked. "I'm afraid my heart is . . .otherwise engaged," I said.

He smiled broadly, a young man's confidence radiating out like the sun's last beams through the purple clouds behind the fort. "Ferrin, I hope you won't be offended," he whispered. "But, as they say in SoHo, I wasn't aspiring that high."

VII

I might have slapped him; perhaps I should have. But the secret was out. It was difficult keeping secrets in Mombasa.

The Bletchley Park contingent knew that I did not normally return to Allidina Visram School until just before
dawn, when Abraham's Shirazi driver would take me back
through the narrow streets below the balconied houses and
along the deserted ring road, then past the dozing sentries of the
King's African Rifles. Weekends I was hardly ever around,
and though I took care to show up at the weekly concert
or the odd birthday party, the school was merely where
I worked, however sleepily. There were probably jokes—
"liaison" had two meanings, after all—and I suffered
the occasional wink, but mostly it was all fetid inference:
Trent-Smith was hardly the only one to proposition me,
merely the boldest. A European woman who slept with
an Indian was fair game. Abraham must have known, of
course, as he knew everything.

"I don't think the vice admiral is happy," he said
one Friday evening at dinner. "One would think he has
better things to think about than my horses."

"You shouldn't judge him," I said. "He's just a man."

"Perhaps, but a powerful one. You know what the
Shirazi say: there is no such thing as a small enemy. How
much more so when it is a large one. He seems compelled
to covet what is mine."

"He thinks you an inadequate guardian of the Marwari."

"I am their only guardian, Joan. He will merely
wish to display them at horse shows, like circus beasts. You
know, I was never a nationalist, but it is possible to understand a Mohandas Gandhi. The British are an inferior race
who have seized power and abuse it, endlessly and without
shame. I am so glad they will be brought down after this war."

"Brought down? You mean, if the Axis—"

"If the Axis win or the Allies. Having saved the
English from the Germans, the Americans will not let

them have back what they once stole. These are vast markets. The Americans will want them. Once geared up for war, they will need to produce for peace. I am not a vengeful man, but if Perfidious Albion were to take a bashing, I would not shed a tear."

He had just made the traditional blessing on the wine, chanting the brief prayer in an unusual sing-song that would have puzzled my parents, for it reflected a Jewish tradition that was alien to them. Salting two pieces torn from a yellow loaf heady with turmeric, he passed the plate to me. As we chewed, only the two of us at one end of his long dining table on the terrace overlooking the old town and the dhows in the harbor shining like triangles of light, he brought up what we had been avoiding since the day we had met.

"Joan darling . . ."

The servants came in, bearing trays of food: vegetable samosas, *nyama choma* of lamb on a bed of pilau, and boiled collard greens, *sukuma wiki*. It was hard to know what his Shirazis thought of this, for on the rare occasions when Abraham's wife came out with the girls, they served her as well. Discrete they were, of course, but bribable. Everyone in Africa was bribable. And not stupid: just as Abraham knew everything that went on in his universe, it was inconceivable that Mrs. Talal did not know what went on in hers. Hindu or Muslim, Christian or Jew, no woman could bear to know that her husband had taken another. Nor could I bear to be that other. The servants withdrew. It would be easier for us both if I spoke first. "It's not a good situation, is it?"

"We're about to spoil a Sabbath meal, aren't we?"

"I told you, I'm never too angry to eat."

"Too hurt, then?"

"I'm a rancher's daughter. I don't hurt easily. And you needn't worry. I make it a point not to cry."

"Will you mind if I do?"

Despite myself, I let go a hard look. I'd wanted more self-control than that. "I'd be surprised if you did, Abraham, whether about the decline of Albion or the decline of us. We've had our fun. Let's leave it at that."

At this, his face drained of color, then as suddenly flushed. "That is unnecessary and untrue, Joan. If I could, I would divorce. You know that."

"You mean, if you could without repercussions."

"My wife is a good woman. She does not deserve to be abandoned. The children do not need the shame."

"Nor do I, Abraham," I said.

"You deserve better than this, my Joan."

"I deserve nothing more than a lift home," I said. "Will you summon your driver, or shall I call a cab?"

VIII

Two weeks later I broke J8. Maybe I could have done it earlier and, theoretically at least, caused the war to end that much sooner. Maybe not. All I know is that I was again working hard and long and with renewed intensity; perhaps I got lucky. There was also much to be learned from the others' progress, so that when the eureka moment arrived I hardly felt triumph, but merely relief. Somewhere in the Indian Ocean or in the Pacific, an American submarine or warplane would soon be bearing down on a Japanese tanker or a freighter carrying ammunition or food for the imperial troops in their island fortresses, or perhaps the very troops themselves. My work would have been part of that, as much so as if I'd pressed the button that released the torpedo or dropped the bomb. I often dreamed of it, colorful melodramatic dreams in which the horror my work had unleashed lived alongside, thrived alongside, the self-satisfaction of success.

"Good show on the ciphers, Ferrin!"

Vice Admiral Lord Braithwaite had finally gotten my name straight. He was grinning, the full ruin of his English dentistry leaping out at me. I thought he might clap my back. "You're being mentioned in dispatches, are you aware?"

"Col. Moseley was good enough to let me know. My job, sir."

"Nonsense. You boffins have turned out a delightful surprise. It's hardly a secret I didn't think any of this would amount to a hill of—Cyril?"

"*Maharagwe*," Albright said.

"*Maharagwe*, beans, *maharagwe*," Braithwaite said, as if he were a boy at school. "Mr. Albright is teaching me useful Swahili, Ferrin. After the war I may come back here, buy a farm. Don't like the coast much. Entirely too hot. But in the highlands, tea, a few cows, *maharagwe*, that sort of thing. India's done. People won't work. Politicized."

"I'm told, Lord Braithwaite, that the British presence in Kenya may be somewhat reduced after the war." I have no idea why I said that. It was as if I were intent on bringing Abraham into the conversation, as though I had absorbed part of him in me—and was now compelled to get him out. "Nationalism, sir."

"Nonsense, Ferrin. The Union Jack will never be struck in East Africa. It may not be fashionable to say so, but your native Kenyan is no . . ." He looked again to Albright.

"*Mzungu.*"

"Yes, of course. I know that one. *Mzungu, wazungu.* Without us *wazungu* they'll come a cropper, and they know it." His tone now changed. "Tell me about my horses, Ferrin."

For some reason, what I was about to say gave me a peculiar kind of physical pleasure, the kind that might be difficult to describe in mixed company. I had been rehearsing my response for days now. I delivered the verdict slowly, spacing out the words. "Your horses, sir, belong to Mr. Talal."

"I know that."

"And he is not giving them up."

"Of course he is, Ferrin. It's just price."

"I don't think so, sir."

"Price, price, price."

"No, your lordship," I said. "No. No. No."

"Don't be cheeky with me, lieutenant. What's a fair price? I don't need them all. One stallion, one mare. It's not the world, is it?"

"You don't have the money, sir."

"I have as much as I require."

"Lord Braithwaite, whatever your offer, it will be refused," I said. "Mr. Talal does not wish to sell to you, or to anyone else. That is conclusive. Consequently, if it pleases your lordship, I should like to request reassignment."

"It doesn't. You may not."

"Sir, I—"

"I don't care what you request, Ferrin. This isn't the bloody RCAF. You'll stand your watch until relieved."

"Sir, I am *mjamzito.*"

"What?"

"*Mjamzito,*" I repeated. "Your lordship."

"What is that? Cyril, what is this girl saying?"

A vacuum opened up in the room, a balloon of silence that grew and grew until finally Albright popped it, as though with a pin. But it was not a pin. It was his tone. "Vice admiral, the lieutenant is saying...."

In whatever language, the phrase had almost certainly never been spoken by a lieutenant to a flag officer of the Royal Navy, and certainly not in Swahili. It took a moment, a long one. Braithwaite looked from Albright to me, then back to Albright, then back to me. Beneath his luxuriant mustache the vice admiral pursed his thin lips, then walked resolutely behind his desk and, heavily, sat. Finally he spoke. "Extraordinary."

"Not really, sir," I said.

"How?"

"The usual way, sir."

"I mean to say, Lieutenant Ferrin, by whom?"

"Your lordship, I'd rather not say."

"One of my officers? I must know."

"No, sir. Not one of your officers."

Braithwaite's eyes now widened in horror. "*Not* an officer? Other ranks?"

"I'd rather not say, sir."

"You'll bloody well say if I order you to, Ferrin. I order you to. What is the name of this man? Are you aware that intimate relations with other ranks is contrary to—" He stopped. "It isn't other ranks, is it?"

"No, sir."

"Oh my God," Braithwaite said. "Albright?"

"*Gombezeka*, sir."

"Speak English!"

"Reprehensible, sir."

"I know that, Cyril. Of course it is. The question is, what must be done about it?"

"It is a military affair, sir," Albright said.

"It is a military-civilian affair, Cyril. And I do believe that is the right word—affair. Is it not, Ferrin?"

"It's over, sir."

"Jolly good," Braithwaite said. "Of course it's over. You're over, Ferrin. I shall have you out of here when your tour is done. I'm ashamed of having you on my staff. Even were I Canadian I would be ashamed. When is your tour done?"

"In six months' time, sir."

"Time enough for court martial."

"On what charges, sir?" I asked. For some reason I was no longer afraid. What could Vice Admiral Sir Hoddings Lord Braithwaite CBE do to me that Abraham had not?

"I don't care what charges, lieutenant. There will be charges. Fraternizing with the enemy, for one thing."

"Mr. Talal is not the enemy, sir." I don't know where I got the nerve. "He is a British subject."

"Fraternizing with a British subject then. Fraternizing with someone. Dereliction of duty. Refusing to obey an order. Absence from post without leave. Don't you worry, Ferrin. Charges there will be if I have personally to rewrite the Admiralty Code."

"Begging your lordship's pardon," Albright said in his quiet way. "You were quite right, sir. There are certain delicate *civilian* aspects to this matter."

"Go on."

"Firstly, we have the question of timing. There are specific, ah, biological manifestations—"

"I'll be showing, sir."

"Indeed, your lordship. So it might be best, to avoid embarrassment all around, for Lieutenant Ferrin to return to the RCAF for reassignment. Her work here is, I understand, done." Albright looked at me oddly, his face almost softening. Later I would understand. "Work done rather well, by all accounts, wouldn't you agree, sir?"

"I am no longer concerned with ciphers," Braithwaite said. Then, in another tone: "What am I not understanding here? You said *firstly*."

"This is a conservative society, your lordship. It's bad enough when we have white members of the military engaging in *uhusinano wa ngono*... sexual relations, as it were—"

"As it were?" Braithwaite exploded. "Cyril, the girl is pregnant!"

"Yes, of course, sir. But when it is a European woman and a non-white person, a *Muhindi*—"

"Would that not be *Seti*, in this case, Mr. Albright?" I said.

Albright reflected. "Yes, of course, lieutenant. *Seti* indeed." He beamed as though I were his student and had caught him out. As if I were his success.

The vice admiral clearly had had enough. "What are you people going on about?"

"*Muhindi*, sir," I said. "It's broadly Indian, Hindu to be precise, though Mr. Talal is not in fact a—"

"Talal be damned," Braithwaite said. "This is not about Talal, or his infernal horses. It is, it is—what is it about, Cyril? Be so good as to cease your dithering. Come out with it!"

"*Seti* designates a wealthy Indian, sir," Albright said. "Lieutenant Ferrin has put her finger right on it. The Indian community would be extremely upset. A.S. Talal is a pillar of that community and, as I say, it is a conservative community. We rather need their cooperation. They would be—"

"*Ubabaifu*," I said. "Upset, sir."

"How *uba*-whatever?"

"Over the short term, unpleasantly sticky, your lordship. Perhaps worse, over time the political situation—"

"What political situation? Do we have a political situation in Kenya on which I've not been briefed?"

"Not so much in Kenya just at the moment, sir. But the Indian community here maintains strong ties with the sub-continent. As you know, there are currents in India–"

"Cyril, are you telling me that something which happens between two persons in the middle of the night— good Lord, I hope it was in the middle of the night—can possibly inspire rebellion in an entire country? That is patently absurd."

Albright seemed to grow taller. He was, after all, a don. And this was his field. "Vice admiral, stranger things have happened. Just at the moment the Indian community, which supplies us with almost all our requirements for food, lodging, tropical clothing, even beer—a good deal of this is in the hands of the very Mr. Talal who—"

"I know who Mr. Talal is, Cyril. I also know I have the power to commandeer all the food and lodging and beer—even beer—we require. Have you forgotten I am God here? I'll have him thrown in Fort Jesus before you can say—what is that word for beans?"

"*Maharagwe,* sir."

"*Maharagwe,* then. And I'll have his horses in the bargain."

Albright coughed gently. "No, sir. I don't think that will do anything but upset the Indian community, which does control commerce in Kenya, in East Africa in fact. This is not a situation which calls for main strength. It calls, sir, for tact."

"I am a vice admiral in His Majesty's Navy, Cyril. We are in a war. What will not be sold us, I will take."

Albright grew taller still, and instead of approaching Braithwaite's desk stepped backward and away, as though to distance himself not only from the vice admiral but from his thinking. "Your lordship, should you choose to punish Lieutenant Ferrin for what can only be considered a human failure, and I think an understandable one in wartime especially, I shall report to the Foreign Office that you are a bumbler and a brute, and if you should go so far as to place in jeopardy British interests by undermining our already sensitive relations with the Indian community of East Africa by pursuing a punitive policy toward one or more of that community for what I can only think of as personal reasons, I shall resign my post forthwith and go directly to Downing Street, with which I have excellent relations, and—should that fail—to the press. You may govern here, vice admiral, but you do not rule. Those days, sir, are over."

IX

Montreal was mild that winter, mild for Montreal, but sub-Arctic compared with the coolest nights in Kilindini, even on Abraham's dhow, when he would wrap his jacket around my shoulders as the wind whipped the normally placid waters of the harbor into miniature whitecaps crisp and pale as meringue.

My teaching schedule was light and spread out over four days in the mornings—the head of the Faculty of Mathematics had been my professor as an undergraduate, and was accommodating in the extreme, perhaps also because most of the good male teachers were called up—and I had a Québécoise nanny who came in those days until 2 PM, so that even when a student kept me after class I was able to walk from the campus to our flat on Prince Albert Street and still have time for lunch before she left.

I was not the only one of the old Bletchley Park contingent who had moved on. By the time the baby came, my former colleagues had been redistributed, redeployed, scattered. The tide of war had turned. Some were removed back to Bletchley Park as our code-breaking activities were more and more integrated with the Americans'. Some followed the return of the Eastern Fleet to the Indian Ocean and the Pacific, where listening stations were again established in Ceylon and China. I was receiving kind, chatty notes from places I had never been.

Though Amanda Hobbes never wrote, apparently not having forgiven me for my indiscretions on the wrong side of the color line, through Jenny Singleton I learned that Trent-Jones, that beautiful brash boy, had been killed, shot down by a Japanese destroyer in the Indian Ocean; that van Oost, the Dutchman who had climbed Kilimanjaro in the first weeks, had put a bullet through his head for no reason anyone knew; that poor stuttering Charlie Fahnstock had been promoted to major; and that to the surprise of all Vice Admiral Lord Braithwaite had proved himself a master strategist, outwitting and outgunning the Japanese in the South China Sea. This last I knew. The Canadian papers were calling him "a second Nelson."

Beyond these notes from friends, all franked by the military and rubber-stamped PASSED BY CENSOR, were two civilian envelopes. The first came when I was still in London, having been transferred back to RCAF headquarters in Lincoln's Inn Fields, where it was decided, in view of my condition, that I should be honorably discharged as a casualty. As such, I may have been the only pregnant officer to be awarded the War Medal, Class B—wounded.

"Dearest Joan," it began,

I would not write and make a bad situation all the more painful but for the fact that I have news that will please you.

According to my contacts, which I view as authoritative, your brother, Group Capt. David Levy Ferrin, RCAF, is currently a prisoner of war, held by the Japanese in a work camp in Thailand, quite near Bangkok. My information is that he is, given the circumstances, in reasonably good health. If your brother is indeed as strong a specimen as you believe, and his walking out of Burma goes quite a long way to vouchsafe this, there is every chance he will survive the war to be reunited eventually with you and with your family.

You may contact him through the Red Cross according to the particulars on the enclosed page. Though the Japanese are not particularly gracious regarding information on the status of prisoners, they will allow packages, not least because they are having a devil of a time feeding themselves, to say nothing of their POWs.

I hope you are well, and that you will forgive me for contacting you, but I thought you would like to know. Please do not feel you must respond. I remain,

Your good friend,
Abraham Talal

At once I made up a package—tinned fish, chocolate, tea, soap, toothbrush and toothpowder, razor blades, and—it was close to Passover—a box of matzah, which I found in a shop in the East End, hoping the Japanese might not grab that, either because it was clearly some sort of religious item or because they simply might not recognize it for the bread it was.

The Red Cross itself was not terribly helpful, merely confirming after some time what had been in Abraham's note. But they did provide a channel for me to send parcels every week while I remained in England, and when I returned to Canada. Of course I never heard from David—the Japanese were uncivilized in that regard—and then after several months the Red Cross admitted they had lost track of him altogether. All over Asia the Japanese were in retreat, and they marched their prisoners with them. Many times it was to tear at me that my success in breaking J8 and thus helping to defeat the Japanese may also have contributed to David's death. After the war, I learned he had stumbled, sick with malaria and gangrene, on a forced march, and been shot.

The second letter carried no return address, but like the first bore civilian stamps and a Mombasa postmark. I received it in Montreal, one month before the birth.

My dear Miss Ferrin,

You may remember me. I was political adviser to Vice Admiral Lord Braithwaite during his tenure as CO East Africa Command here in Mombasa, which the military called Kilindini Station and which, as you may know, is all but abandoned, the war having moved on.

As have you.

I understand from a certain source that you are safely back in Canada, and gainfully employed (which is rather more than I can say for myself—I long for the day I am back at Oxford!). Furthermore I understand that you are well along in your pregnancy, and I trust that this too is proceeding well.

I hope you will forgive me therefore for my impertinence in suggesting that should the occasion arise, you may wish to contact a person in Montreal with regard to arranging for a certain ceremony which in Swahili is called tohara *(alternatively:* jando*). As I doubt you have reason to keep up your study of this language in Canada, I should say the best translation would be "bris."*

As I never married, and thus have no children (I'm so sorry if this may seem a backhanded insult; I mean no harm), I have no direct experience of arranging a circumcision. Certainly I did not arrange my own.

It is just that I feel a certain paternal pleasure in knowing, especially with the news from Europe, that another little Jew will shortly be coming into the world. Or perhaps it is that because my own life has been compromised—to speak boldly, it has been a lie—I would like to think I have been helpful in setting the child on a better path.

Please find on the enclosed sheet the name of a reliable rabbi and the name of the rabbi in London who suggested him.

I hope you will forgive me for not having been honest with you in Mombasa, but I'm afraid my life has been lived in a different time, under different circumstances.

Please then accept my warmest regards for yourself and the child. Mazel tov!

Your friend,
Cyril Albright

P.S. If it is a girl, you may wish to contact the same rabbi. I believe it is the tradition to name a girl child in the synagogue, but I am unaware of how this is done. If your child is indeed a girl, I trust she will be as brave and forthright as her mother, whom I will admire until my dying day.

David Abraham Ferrin was born on an unseasonably warm November afternoon in Montreal, and in accordance with Jewish law was circumcised eight days later by the rabbi suggested by Cyril Albright. My university colleagues assumed the David Ferrin I sometimes mentioned was my husband, dead in the war—society, even the raffish society of Montreal academia, in those days frowned on unwed mothers. I never lied; they inferred. My own mum and dad, changed irrevocably since the death of their only son, tired now and worn, deduced that Abraham was the father's name, and convinced themselves that he too was a casualty of war. I let them all think what they would. I should have liked to name my baby David Cyril. But the Jewish tradition is to name a child for the dead.

The Man
Who Kissed
Stalin's Wife

To be saddened by loss is better than to be saddened by gain. In 1935, when my country was cannibalizing itself and the civilized world preparing for war, those who knew better sent me to the South Seas. Armed only with *The Collected Marx and Lenin* on onionskin, the Nagan revolver which had been presented to me upon acceptance to the Zhukovsky Advanced Aeronautical Academy, and an introduction to an Irishman in Papeete, I sailed out from Vladivostok in a drizzle to arrive at Tahiti still in a fog.

The Irishman's name was Timothy Tranck. In the nation where scientific socialism ruled, he would long since have been broken down to be processed anew. But on the main road of Papeete, he dealt in spirits and bought and sold the precious commodities of copra and pearl, between dealings with others mumbling sedition to himself. *Tranck Tane*, read the sign above his shop: Mr. Tranck's. He made an odd sympathizer to our cause, but so did I. Together we shared hope and hopelessness like bookends, and between those placed the red-jacketed volumes which spoke our pride. But if I had been exiled from hell to sit out the years until the war in safety, while in my homeland thousands of the democratic underground burned at Stalin's cold stake, it was Tranck's misfortune to have found in paradise not enough.

"You may picture me," he would say, "jumpin' out of the poisonous galley of that wind-jammin' man-killer and fallin' by the grace of God into a grove of coconuts, with roast pig, breadfruit and oranges for breakfast, deejunee and dinner. The Emerald Isle the devil! 'Twas Tahiti the Tor-na'an-Og, with no bogs nor peat, no stir-about and no damned peeler to move you on, no soggarth to tell you you're a sinner."

Understanding the man was never easy for me. My English was as rudimentary really as his, which combined his native jolt and tickle with the sing-song and slang of the southern seas. But his disappointment I understood well enough, and was to know more. "Oh," he would tell me, "I was that attracted by the pretty girls, the trees, and the foine-smelling flowers, that the old man of the ship never could draw me back to the pans of the galley. To be flunky of the kitchen of a windjammer, peelin' pratties, waiting on sailor men! No, the father of a darlin' hid me out by Fautaua Falls, and the jondarmy hunted and hunted and got nothin' for their trouble. But now . . ."

But now. The present is hardly sufficient for any man. Yet, looking back on those times I realize that for me it was, then, nearly enough. I had learned in my native Leningrad, where all roads of the revolution met and began, that the task of the Soviet Man was to make the present stretch into the future in an unbroken red ribbon of works. In the Marquesas, a more perfect past was to intervene. At

Tranck's I studied in French the only practical grammar of Marquesan—written in 1857 by a Monsignor Dordillon, missionary of the Sacré-Coeur. But even within this work, the valor of a past greater than any present ruled. For by then little but a remnant of pure Polynesian was left, the finer meanings having been whittled away in the adhesion of the words of the whites, the adverbs and degrees of comparison lost altogether. The dictionary I worked with was printed in Boston, America, in 1848, and is called *A Vocabulary of the Nukahiwa Language; including a Nukahi-wa-English Vocabulary and an English-Nukahiwan*, but no living Nukahiwan, or Marquesan, could make much of it now. I have read it through, and I have lived among the Marquesans. It makes as much sense against the wretched reality we call the present as does Engels' withering-away state against the Soviet monumentalism. Only a true believer could make the necessary connection. The good cleric Dordillon may have noted that the term for cook is *onata tunu kai*, but the Marquesan calls him, after the white sailors, *kuki*, and *oli mani*, the corruption of "old man," is used for anything broken or blunt—an *oli mani* knife, a ragged pair of trousers or a chipped tooth. The clergy are called *mitinanie*—an effort at missionary—for there was no such thing before, and *hatetie* is chastity, which no one knew. Little remains unchanged. The stamp of English is upon these seas, and even the French officers of Marquesan-manned schooners are forced to use it. It is the language of capitalism, of course, in which Marx himself grew adept, as did I.

But when finally I went out with my new knowledge and old prejudices on Tranck's schooner to sow the seed of socialism on the atoll where the Irishman's only child lived in a paradise enforced, I wooed her not in the desic-cated Marquesan, the empty pidgin English or the Tahitian

French she and I well understood, but in the language I had learned at my mother's knee in Leningrad, then Petrograd, before that St. Petersburg. And in the warm nights as I lay upon my pallet looking upon her solemn beauty beneath the Southern Cross, murmured to her "*Vperiod i vyshe, vperiod i vyshe*," words whose association she could scarcely have understood. *Forward and upward* indeed! It had been the name of a periodical in Leningrad. A Russian, according to the proverb, is like a dray horse; no matter how far he has been driven, or how heavy the load, his thoughts turn ever back to the bare, cold stable he calls home. But of that home I was to know little enough.

Though each fortnight I sat in my hut, or in Goetz's store, to inscribe the Cyrillic letters as earlier generations of Russians had scratched icons upon bare wood, no return letter came for me on the mail steamer which anchored beyond the outer reef only long enough for the trader to deliver his canvas sack, marked with the *tricolore,* and receive another in exchange. If the mail was not getting through I could bear that, for as a cadet at the Zhukovsky I had learned stoicism in the face of deprivation. But if my mother, for some reason, was no longer there to receive it, this would be far worse. As it was, even before my sudden departure, we had not heard from my brother Leonid for weeks. Like so many others in those times, he had simply disappeared, but we had not given up hope. Why had my mother not replied? I dared not write anyone else, and was left only with the most perverse of hopes: the more thoroughly the NKVD opened and destroyed the mails, the better the chance my mother was safe. Beyond this fortnightly rite I had little time to reminisce. Tranck's island was made for work. My months in the lushness of Papeete had hardly prepared me for the desolation I would find.

Then, Tranck had spent his time driving me out to his thriving coconut plantations, instructing me in the copra trade and revealing to me the secrets he had acquired— stolen, most likely—of the new science of pearl. I learned to dive, to appraise and trade, and spent long hours with the microscope in Tranck's laboratory, learning to set nacre about the speck in its shell. Tranck's optimism infected me, and when he said, "A pearl's not unlike a man, Grisha. The way 'tis set so 'twill grow," I realized I was giving myself over to his dreams the way I had sat up long nights at the Zhukovsky absorbing Yuriev, Kulebyakin, Tupolev, Vechinikin, Ushakov, Stechkin, Mikulin, Klimov, Mussinyants and the seminal theories of Zhukovsky himself. I had hardly to ask myself what, for instance, had the Kutta-Zhukovsky Theorem of Aerodynamical Lift in common with the "borrowed" principles of the Japanese, Kokichi Mikimoto, of nurturing and harvesting the pearl. It was as simple as this: if we at the Zhukovsky and the other academies—the Frunze in Moscow, the Red Banner at Monino, the Voroshilov Naval Academy in Leningrad—were concerned with building Soviet military power to withstand the test of whatever war might come, in Papeete I studied with the same diligence the science of pearl to preserve for the abandoned atoll of Atu-Hiva its small share in the world to be.

"What the damn mishes has done to Tahiti," Tranck said to me on board his schooner, sighing as I had many times heard him sigh as he spoke these words, "We won't let it happen to Atu-Hiva, will we, lad? Goetz has been my government up to now, and it's only luck that drove the damned penguins from my sand. But now you're to be in charge, I needn't have no fears. If Goetz is administration, you must be inspiration. I've instructed him he's not your boss, that you must work side by side."

"And in case of dispute?"

"In true socialism there is no dispute between the government and the party."

Where had he heard that? He said these words with all the conviction I had put into a similar phrase: *vlast truda*, the rule of labor. Had I not written a verse and recited it on the occasion of my group's promotion from Pioneers to Comsomol, the All-Union Lenin Communist League of Youth?

> *In the great parade*
> *Of the forces of the Soviet Union*
> *My tread*
> *Clearly rings out!*

But I had been only sixteen. "And in dispute?"

"You may mediate among yourselves," he said. "Have you no experience of mediation in your Soviet Union?" He could not have noticed my smile, for he was shielding his eyes from the sun, searching the horizon as we sailed. "'Twas the mishes that done it. Before their comin', before the whites and their poison of sin, on these islands was makers of war-fleets, brawlers true, and men. Men, damn it! And so they shall be again. We'll make our Soviet state right here!" He turned to me there on the deck. "You'll see no *behine mako* on my isle, lad, no whores and no booze. When there was natural pearls in that lagoon, they'd go down dead drunk and come up plain dead. But more than that, it ate their gut. They can't hold it as you and I, Grisha, and they've more to be sorrowful for. Ah, they was beautiful women and brawling men then. To look into the face of Seventh Man you can see them as they were, though now for moroseness you can't do better than he. Just keep him off the juice, lad. For yourself I've packed a demi-john below, but be careful drinkin' there alone. Do no man to quaff to his own beat, and 'twill make you sad as them. There! D'you see?"

From the deck, I barely saw the speck. It was easy to understand why Tranck had chosen this spot; for beyond the mail steamer on the fortnightly run to Ha-o two hundred miles to the east, not even a captain completely lost would deem it worth the stop. Low and flat, it seemed to melt into the sea itself, and only when we were just on top, riding through the break in the inner reef in the ship's boat, could it be seen for what it was.

Tranck was as excited as a boy. "Sure we could blast a passage through the coral to the lagoon. But if we did, there'd be no end of captains sloggin' rum, tradin' trinkets for pearl, buyin' the women with snips of cloth and payin' off their husbands in booze. 'Tis the history of these seas, lad, and I've seen it almost from the first. Seventh Man, his father made regular practice of eatin' his enemies down to the toe. Look around and you'll find heaps of skulls hidden away. But now. . . hell, lad, they don't bother no more hardly with the *tapus*, much less tattooin'—that was an art!– or their dyin' tongue. Language fattens with use, Grisha, and theirs years back was bone."

This discourse I had heard many times, many nights. Tranck had long since become used to ordering his world according to his views. But the man I saw step ashore at the tiny rock quay was hardly the sharp trader of Papeete, dealer in spirits, copra-grower, initiator of the culture of pearl, nor Marxist either. It was as father, a worried parent, that he now appeared, and while a few Atu-Hivans had drifted down to see him in, he ignored us all and caressed the girl, hugging and squeezing her, peering into her eyes that were a copy of his own, leaf green, shameless with soft longing as would any Russian mother be for her own son.

As shameless as myself, for when I lifted my eyes from this scene I saw not the store, the spire of a plank church, outriggers strung out in a line along the beach, a paint-peeling cutter half at anchor, half submerged in the violet lagoon, but my own mother's home—her poor artifacts and memories, my father's picture in its tin frame, the first and last I knew of him, for he had died during the Civil War in Ordzhonikidze's Eleventh Red Army fighting General Denikin's Whites. Even as I shook hands with Tranck's trader Goetz and the oddly pale chief in his filthy pareu, Seventh Man, my heart's eyes were elsewhere.

"Grisha!"

I turned to Tranck, and then followed his gaze. From down the shallow hill which rose from the beach came two figures dressed alike—black coats, wing collars, knotted ties, and upon their heads black felt hats such as I had never seen. "The bloody mishes've come back," he said. "I'll have no sky-pilots on my sand!" He seemed about to explode. "Malachites," he said at last, apparently able to tell one sect from the next on sight, and then turned back to me and changed his tone; now it was as soft and formal, as one moment before it had been brittle with hate. "Pleased I am, Grisha, to present to you my daughter, the finest maiden of the Marquesas, whose mother I loved with a passion, lad. You may take her and love her, but never abuse her. For if you do, I shall have your heart in my hand and wring it dry."

The girl was young, perhaps sixteen, but fully grown and plump in the manner of these seas. Yet there was something about her—beyond her green eyes and the absolute stillness in which she stood—that bespoke a life shattered somehow. Perhaps I recognized in her too the sadness of exile. Lust and compassion battled within me, and then, as I blushed and she turned away, the stronger won. Her name was At Peace. Me they were to call *Pupinay*, which means leprous as well as fair.

★

Of that day and of the next, a Sunday, when Tranck sailed, I remember hardly anything at all. I felt as abandoned as when my mother had told me as a child that my father was dead in the bloody see-saw of Reds and Whites. But then I'd had the emotionalism of the Russian personality within which to withdraw—the opportunity to act the man and comfort my shrieking mother, to vow silent revenge against Denikin's White Guards, to spin out my days in the most unsettled and unsettling of times. In the Russia of those days, to be an orphan was as much honor as loss. It was on Atu-Hiva that I felt bereaved. For companion and guide I had only Goetz, who insisted upon affixing to me my rank: mixed homage, for it was the schooner captain who first despoiled these seas.

"You are not the first white man they have seen, Captain Zabrodny," he said that first evening. He had a larder stocked with Patzenhoffer, and we knocked back several bottles apiece. "In Hamburg I never considered myself being something special—a white. But for them, color means a great deal. I have seen the child of Marquesan mother and white father fall ill at being called a *kanaque* within a group of whites. You must go to Papeete to see truly how they have been shamed. Are you interested, captain, in the theory of race?"

"But why do they not return my greetings and avert their eyes?" I told him how at daybreak I had followed a sweet smell to where two bakers were mixing coconut milk and flour, and wrapping that in palm leaves to bake over a mild fire. All the while I stood there I was ignored, as though my own being were so separate from theirs that I scarcely existed at all.

"They are not used to you."

But this did not satisfy. I had seen them do the same with Goetz, and he had been on this island for years. Tranck had brought him out from Papeete, where the German's company had sent him as an experienced man in goods and finance to wring a settlement from a recalcitrant account. Goetz acquitted himself well and built the debtor's existing stocks into a carefully managed inventory, riding out in chartered schooners to those islands far off the sea roads which the larger traders barely touched, where any bangle, any swatch of cloth, was worth a fortune in copra and the occasional pearl. It was on these smaller atolls, which the French administration in Papeete was hard put to watch, that the law of the *rehu*, the limited diving season, was ignored, and the pearls had given out, though the rare find might still buy the treadle sewing machine of which every Marquesan woman dreamed. With it she could sew the clothes her mother had never needed to catch or hold a man. The missionaries had forbidden nudity and paved the way for the traders' wares; with the legs all but covered, tattooing was stopped, the production of *tapa*, the ingenious beaten bark cloth of the South Seas, forgotten. Those flowery *pareus* Gauguin had captured were spun in New England mills from Virginian cotton, stitched together in the Marquesas on Singer's machines that were bought for fortunes in the pearls which adorned the windows of New York shops, Parisienne throats. Though I might have seen Goetz as nothing more than a rank capitalist who had run from Germany clutching hopes he would return with wealth, Tranck had told me enough to turn any loathing to the same pity I felt for myself. We were exiles both. Every *franc* Goetz put away went for the support of his aged parents in Hamburg. It was hardly conceivable that he would return to see them with enough saved to justify his flight.

That was the first evening. On the second, I heard a muted singing and made my way to the missionaries' church.

Beneath a roof of corrugated tin sat ten women and three men—the number was to grow—their voices raised in an ancient chant that was at once transcendent in lyric as earthbound in form, the awkward mix of the missionaries' hymn with their old chants. It was hardly a blend. The moans of physical longing or the call to war saw no meeting place with any upwards urge. When I entered, they rapidly dispersed, leaving me standing at the back, facing the two Malachites. The name of one was William Lloyd; his partner Lloyd something else. I would keep them apart in my head only by thinking just one seemed to have a tongue. The other never said a word. Both were farmers from the American west, honest and raw, volunteers who had come out to this furthest place as part of a tithe.

"We don't have no regular preachers, you see," William Lloyd said to me. "We're not them Mormons, what pays folks to take up the cloth. They'd like as not pay for souls."

What must they have thought of me? That first day when, like frigate birds, they had appeared to Tranck's gaze and fearlessly displayed a carefully folded letter, replete with wax seal—their *permis from Monsieur l'Inspecteur des Établissements Français de l'Océanie*—they had asked me straight out what my business was to be. Like all clerics, they regarded where they stood as ground made holy at least by that, as perhaps it was, for their presence on Atu-Hiva was as voluntary as mine was forced.

I could not suppress the secularist rage drilled into me as a child, and in which I still believed. "To bring socialism to Atu-Hiva, Mr. Tranck has brought me," I said, and immediately saw that in their eyes I had grown horns, a spade beard. Was William Lloyd peering behind me for evidence of a tail? If so, this he managed to conceal. "We are all God's children, Mr. Zabrodny. We must all get along."

"Except with the Mormons?"

"The Mormons ain't rational in their religion," he said, fingering the black knot of his tie. "You take a *kanaque*, scare the Catholicism out of him, clothe his naked body and what you got? A Mormon. But we of the Malachite Church of the Latter Day Saints give full value straight off. We got the direct line. When the French clamped down the Mormons turned tail, but we come back. We give a good accounting and that's why we're liked, Mr. Zabrodny. Good business pays off. We got two new members this week, paying dues." I suppose he caught my look. "All the poor folks has got is coconuts, of course, but we believe the Lord understands and has taken from those that has sinned and given to us that has not. You wait and see. These islands will soon be cleansed."

So Tranck was not alone in his hopes. "And then?"

"And then there'll be electric light, and automobiles, and proper roads." The missionary's eyes moved beyond me.

A *kanaque* stood in the doorway. I had been seeing him from my first moments on the atoll, though never this close. He was huge, with arms big around as my own thigh. In his hand he held a heavy stick, on his face a hard and unsatisfied look. His name was Tepia a Tevu—Turtle Eggs—and on Atu-Hiva he kept the peace. Tranck had bade him watch, and this he did, pursuing me with a literalness impressive as his bulk and that great stick.

"Turtle Eggs?" Goetz said that night. "He is just to stop the drink. They'll drink, these *kanaques*, and then they are not worth . . ." He finished pouring out the bottle of Patzenhoffer his Marquesan "wife" had brought. "Once, you know, they owned these seas, sharing them only with the wind and rain. But now by disease and misfortune they have been diminished, and by religions which do not suit their simple needs. The best died in battle, captain, or of grief. We can let them drown in alcohol, of course, but how sad to slap them with the one insult past pain. Captain, these are barely men. We must build them up."

"I thought Mr. Tranck brought *me* here for that, not you."

"These are Mr. Tranck's wishes, Captain Zabrodny. Mr. Tranck knows best what must be for his atoll."

"His?" I said. "There flies the *tricolore* night and day, from your very roof...."

Goetz waved his hand.

"And of Seventh Man—is he not chief?"

"*Monsieur le chef?*" Saying that he said all. It was the appellation the French used for their cooks.

"Herr Goetz, how long have you been here?"

"Seven years. Nine in these seas."

"Do you then not know the meaning of the term dictatorship of the proletariat? Are you familiar with the works of Karl Marx? Of Lenin?"

"The papers rarely reach this far, captain," he said. "But I have some idea of what you and Tranck are about."

"And do you, knowing the *kanaka*, think we shall succeed?"

Goetz paused. "Here nothing will succeed," he said.

Yet his pessimism gave me hope. And that night, as the wind whistled through the ill-fitting wood slats of my shack, I poured myself a first long drink from Tranck's demi-john and resolved the next morning to set to work. But no sooner was I abed on the thin pallet I had built up on the dirt floor did the door open slowly. I heard a light footstep cross within. Reaching under the pile of my clothes, I drew out the service pistol which had come to be my most treasured possession. Even now, so far away, often do I waken in a nighttime sweat thinking that in a moment of anguish or fear I might have killed At Peace.

Perhaps it would have been better for her if I had: with her green eyes and dark skin, she was more than *kanaka*, and something less. The combination made her frightening somehow, ghostlike: in her, too, the memory of a better past lived on.

That night was an introduction for me to a passion I had never considered to exist. Like others of my age, I had been indoctrinated in a sexual, as well as a political, dogma. Moscow and Leningrad women, even in the highest circles in which I traveled, were hardly sensual creatures at all. Softness in a woman had become counter-revolutionary two decades before, and our poverty was dire. But the Atu-Hivans were poorer than we. Here beauty was not accident, but practice—as moderation might be, or political vigilance. Only once before had it occurred to me that a woman might have sexual feelings other than those attendant in the simple bartering of her soul. Now the romantico-socialist babblings we had practiced upon the objects of our desire became suddenly as inexplicable as some foolish and exhausted tradition. In reality, this was the case. In matters of love the *ancien regime* lived on, endlessly modified by the political truth of the day. In that Russia under Stalin, the Russia I had fled to arrive in a paradise of endless sensuality, only one woman had embodied for me the highest ideal of what a woman—as woman—might be, and I had met her only twice, both times at official functions. She was not the soft odalisque of Atu-Hiva, but she was real, and it disturbed me that it was she I thought of while I made love to and was made love to by At Peace. Her name was Nadezhda Alleluyeva, and she had had the bad fortune to have married the wrong man. She was Stalin's wife.

★

It was in the early spring of 1931 that we first met, at an evening party to which I had been invited at the Commercial Academy, where she was a student in the chemistry faculty. There was a concert of sorts, an ad hoc series of entertainments put on by the students themselves. Afterward I was taken by friends to the party bureau room, where I found a small company of men and women relaxing in armchairs and chatting quietly, none of whom I knew. I was introduced to a woman, about thirty, with a rather large yet shapely nose and short hair brushed back from the forehead in a manner which accentuated this. Far from being unattractive, it was the kind of honesty which was her mark, of the same sort which no doubt was to cause her sudden and mysterious death. She held out her hand, saying simply, "Alleluyeva," and I remember my knees becoming weak.

"Zabrodny," I had said.

At Peace smoothed the hair from my face. "Did you love her that first night?"

"Never."

"Did she not like you then?"

How to explain the paradox of romantic love, the frustration of being far from one's adored, and yet loving that?

"Be careful of him," the woman next to Alleluyeva had cried. "He is a heart-eater!" She was the wife of one of the generals who by 1937 would be dead.

"Are you a heart-eater?" At Peace asked, and sometimes thereafter would tease me, murmuring "Captain Heart-Eater" as she stroked my face or we practiced *honi*, which the missionaries in their ignorance had described as rubbing noses, but which was simply an exchange of scent. Captain Heart-Eater. I was not much of a heart-eater then. I was shocked at how human and accessible Nadezhda Alleluyeva could be at the very period when her husband was closing himself in with his delusions. She herself opposed him at almost every point, until in November of 1932 it became too much. As early as 1929, when Bukharin, Rykov and Tomsky were condemned—the famous Buryto grouping—she openly showed her sympathy, and made no secret of her respect for Bukharin in particular. It must have enraged Stalin even then.

"But why did she remain with him?"

"I don't know," I said. "She was the mother of his children."

"She might have taken them away. I do not think she was as brave as you say."

"In my country, to speak is to be brave."

"You must take me to that atoll," she said. "I shall speak. I am not afraid."

"The hand of Tranck Tane will not protect you there, my sweet."

"Then yours will."

"I was hard put to protect myself," I told her. But I am certain she could not have understood. For almost ten years I had daily risked my life as part of the amorphous and ultimately powerless resistance known as the democratic underground—in Stalin's terms, the deviation of the right. I had been told so many times that it was better to work from within that in many ways I had forgotten what it was to be bold. Still, it *was* better to work from within. It hardly made sense to die. "At Peace," I said, "who is the policeman of this atoll?"

"Tepia a Tevu," she said.

"If Tepia a Tevu, if Turtle Eggs, wished to hurt you, who would stop him?"

"Why would he wish that?"

"Let us say that your interests and his were not compatible."

"But I have not known him to have any interests."

"His interests are to protect this atoll from alcohol."

"Because it is bad for the people," she said.

"And if the people want it?"

"They should not want something which is bad."

I do remember that night. Before dawn it had rained, so that the sea air seemed to part away. "Have you loved before?" I took the courage to ask.

"With many," she replied.

I suppressed my horror, for by our standards, those of an enlightened Soviet society, At Peace would be nothing more than a whore. "But have you *loved*?"

"I do not know what that is."

"A man—" to stay with, I would have said. But it was not enough.

"He would have to be a man then," she said. "There have been none here. He could not be French, for I hate them for what they have done to my mother's race. He could not be Marquesan, for there are none left that are men." She looked at me with a dread beyond her years. "That is why my father brought you. He said that you are a man who has read books, and is honest and strong, and that if you become one with this island you will be my husband, and father children by me, and have Atu-Hiva for your own."

"Is that the bridal price?" I asked, making it a joke. "How is it all believe Tranck Tane rules this land? It is French."

She waved her hand and proceeded to educate me in the ways of the South Seas. She told how her father had acquired the atoll from the Tahitian dentist, Porter, because it was famed in the annals of the *a'riori*, the ancient minstrels, as a place of orgiastic dancing, a retreat to which the old aristocracy retired to rest, and where the noblewomen could sit beneath the shade of the banyans and let their skins whiten again. But the royal family of Tahiti had fallen into the dentist's debt, and for so many gold fillings and facings, for so much bridgework and extraction, they had bartered away the isle. Porter found it planted with thousands of coconut trees and planted thousands more, only to discover his commercial venture endangered by a plague of ship-borne rats which, with no natural enemies, grew without limit, feeding upon the copra crop. He sold the atoll to Tranck. "It is my father's," At Peace said. "As one day it will be mine." She said this as haughtily as any woman of these islands might. For even had she one hundred brothers, Marquesan inheritance follows the female line. It was clear she was making me a bargain I would be fool to turn down.

But her pride, together perhaps with her youth and sullen beauty, rankled me. "Does this atoll not belong to the people who live here?" I asked. "Those whose fathers and grandfathers are buried here, who were here before your father came to these seas?"

She laughed. "Before my father there were only guardians here. This place was *tapu*, kept for the Tahitian chiefs who visited only from time to time."

"Surely all these people going about haven't sprung up from the sea."

She continued looking at me as does a child when an adult has done some foolish thing. "But my father brought them," she said. "Did you not know? Just as he brought the cats."

"The cats?"

"To eat the rats," she said. "My father collected all the stray cats of Tahiti and brought them here to eat the rats."

"But I haven't seen any rats."

"Because the cats ate them all, my darling. First they ate the rats and when there were no more they ate themselves; the stronger, the weaker . . ."

"The swifter, the slower; the brighter, the duller," I found myself saying. It was the Russian proverb I had learned as a child.

"Until there came a day when only two cats were left," she said.

"And one ate the other, and that one starved."

"Yes, yes. And then my father brought people from all the islands to live here and be peaceful as in the old times, and work the copra, and bring up the pearls until those gave out, and be free of the bad ways. Missionaries followed, but he sent them away."

"They would tell the people there was a God more mighty than Tranck," I said.

"The missionaries frighten the people. They create sin."

"And does not Tranck Tane create sin? He has his Tepia a Tevu."

"That is just to keep them from drink," she said with all the innocence in the world. "If they drink they will not work, and if they do no work they will die."

Had not her father told her his charity alone supported the atoll? "I should think if that were the case, they would gladly work and any drinking they did would not prevent that."

"If they drink, they become sad."

"I should think they may be induced to work," I said.

"Will you threaten them with your gun?"

"I will not threaten anyone."

"Then they will not work," she said.

✳

He who believes strongly is bound eventually to come face-to-face with the limits of his belief. I had argued with Tranck that socialism might be brought to Atu-Hiva without tears, that from the revolutionary past in the Soviet Union we might take lesson, not example. But when I called upon Seventh Man and found him sitting before a palm-frond hut, a stack of dominoes before him on a table of rough deal, my hopes suddenly fell. If to Tranck he appeared noble, to me he was burnt out, a shell. I called out a greeting in English, and for good measure a Russian curse, for he barely noted my arrival, and remained surly as impatiently he heard me out.

"First the *Catorika*, then the *Mormoni* and the *Protestani* and the *Malachiti*," he said. "And now this *Marax*. We do not need any of it."

"Because Tranck Tane provides you with tinned foods, with cotton and with flour for bread."

He shrugged. "Tranck Tane makes his profits. We dived for him when there was pearl. I do not believe there will be pearl again. We bring him copra now."

"It is meager and spoiled," I said. At this he turned his head, and as he did so, his *pareu* fell open, exposing his private parts. I was immensely embarrassed, for him as well as myself, so that when he turned back it was I who was forced to avert my eyes. "Do you see no greater future for your people than to subsist upon charity? Tranck has made of this atoll a zoological garden, Seventh Man. Do you know what that is?"

"A white cannot insult me, Pupinay Captain," he said, and with that rose and turned back into his hut. There was no door. For a moment he stopped and faced me, almost spitting out the words. "When my people knew the legends and lived fully as men, the whites were cowering in caves. You have nothing to teach."

"Nothing to teach?" I shouted back, but he was already inside. "Look at this, your island. Look at your poor and dispirited people. Look at yourself!"

But Seventh Man had looked too long at himself, I am sure, and had no need of more. He did not come out, nor did he reply. With heavy heart I walked back to Goetz's store. There I found the trader handing over a stack of tins to a woman of middle years. Her *pareu* was clean, and though she was fat and no longer attractive, she wore a flower in her hair. Somehow it set off her face. I was amazed to see in it a shrewdness I had thought did not here exist. Perhaps the best had died, but survival is something too. Goetz scratched a number in his great green ledger and turned to me. "I shall spare you the misery," he said. "They will not work. Not for you, not for me, not for Tranck. Even the missionaries have a time of it. You have only to look at their church."

Their plain hall was as battered and neglected as any building on the atoll. "But why?"

Goetz shrugged. "Myself, I believe it is the race which has died. Simply died, captain. There are races and races."

"There are only men," I said. "I shall want some tools." With these the next morning I began.

My first task was to make some sense of the coconut plantation, cutting out the older non-bearing trees, hauling them down to the beach to burn, thinning out the volunteer shoots, cleaning out from under the remaining trees the rubble of the years, rusted tin cans, broken bottles and jars, rotted nail-studded boards no one had thought to preserve. On the entire island there was not one wheeled conveyance—these would hardly have been practical in the sand—and so I hauled the refuse by myself, brutal work, but less brutal by far than the mental strain. Though I had not had to labor with my back for a long time, I had always remained in the same physical trim that had been one of the requirements for entrance to the Zhukovsky. At the very time of my leaving the Soviet Union I had been on special duty at the Summer Air Forces Camp near Serpukhovo, about two hours by motor from Moscow, and so it was that I had spent the season before in strenuous physical activity. Even in Papeete I had not neglected my body, but had run and swum every day. Now, working like a *muzhik* in the sun, the strain was not on my body, for while my hands bled, then hardened, my mind drifted back to the days of my life in the Soviet Union, as over and over I recreated that one moment when my fate had been given over to the bizarre obsessions of Tranck.

A civilian friend had come out to Serpukhovo and we met outside the camp, purposively mingling with the bathers in the River Oka. His message was as brief as it was grim: all branches of the democratic underground were to dissolve at once and wait for better times.

The news of this collapse left me seething, but there was little I could do, and less so shortly thereafter when, in Leningrad, Sergei Mironovich Kirov, the butcher who had turned my lovely native city into a barracks, was assassinated in his party headquarters at the former Smolney Institute. This act provided Stalin with all he would need. Within hours arrests were made all over the Soviet Union—the NKVD head, Yagoda, himself shipped off for trial and replaced by Medved who, a fortnight later, was replaced as well. The whole of the country was in an uproar of speculation and fear. Yet within this, at its very heart, a peculiar calm reigned.

When I was ushered into the office of Yakov Ivanovich Alksnis, head of the Soviet Air Forces and member of the Revolutionary Military Council of the Republic, that calm was such that one would not have known that all about us the Soviet Union seemed intent on cannibalizing itself. Though during the terror Alksnis devoted himself to protecting his junior officers from arrest, he was not long able to protect himself. In 1937 he was labeled a traitor, broken to the ranks, tortured and then shot. It was Alksnis who ordered me to fly at once to Odessa and report for instructions there. In a time of great fear I knew instinctively that he was that rare *horoshy chelovek*, a decent fellow who would not play according to the depraved rules of the time.

Willingly I flew to Odessa and thence on to Vladivostok, where I caught a steamer for Papeete. Others in danger at the Zhukovsky were sent on similar missions in order to preserve them from Stalin's wrath. Alksnis knew that the young guard of the air corps must be preserved, and so Musabekov disappeared into the North Ossetian Republic to oversee meteorological information; Kushnitzov envoyed to China as air attaché; Shprinz to Brazil, and Zhuavlyov, the test pilot who had been injured in the breaking in of the famed ANT-14, packed off to

North Africa on a mysterious mission having to do with the technology of wine. Wine! Just as Stalin had prepared his terror long before the Kirov murder, so had the leaders of the democratic opposition prepared our tactical withdrawal. Alas, it was the leadership that did not survive. By the time I had induced the Marquesans to work for themselves, Alksnis was dead, though I did not know it then. For I had not received one letter from home. It was hardly difficult to suspect the worst. Being so far away I felt a kind of shame.

All through that year I worked the plantation alone, with no company other than Goetz—who thought me stupid—and At Peace, her father's child—who thought me mad for not shooting one or two of her people for their scorn. There were more than enough about to shoot, for everywhere I worked a silent group would gather to watch me toil. So much for socialism by example. When these were absent there was always Tepia a Tevu, making certain he knew where I was every moment of every day. Oh, how I wished to be home, to see my aged mother, to have some news of Leonid, perhaps for only a moment to take leave of the harsh world and go out to visit the simple grave in the Novodevichy Cemetery, the last resting place of Nadezhda Alleluyeva. It was not I who had been the heart-eater, but she.

★

When Stalin's grandfather had been a serf, the Marquesans had been socialists for centuries, their chiefs *primo inter pares* when any fancy of the tsar was God's will. They had been cooperators who thought nothing of personal property when trade in black slaves had been legal in Europe, and honorable too, democrats whose state had not needed to wither away, for it had never existed. But now . . .

Though I had resisted the theories of Goetz and the advice of Tranck, I knew now hope alone could not rekindle what was lost.

"They are hardly the best of what once was," the trader said as we paddled out beyond the outer reef to meet the fortnightly packet bound for Ha-o. "There is a science of cultural genetics—you may have heard of this? I can show you the studies of Freilvacher and Krohn. Fact." He exchanged the mail sack in which I had placed my letter with an identical one marked with the *tricolore*. It was empty, save for a periodical from Berlin, *Der Stürmer*, an anti-Semitic tract whose value to Goetz in a Jewless place I could not see. We wrestled aboard two cases of Patzenhoffer and a demi-john, and made for the quay. By the time we beached I had decided there was little sense in putting off what must be.

It was a Sunday. I could hear the *himene* from the Malachite church. With At Peace I walked down the smooth shore, the water of the lagoon a violet of incomparable purity. Together we entered the crowded church. As though on signal, the *himene* ceased. The two preachers had done their work well, gathering up what stray souls there were. When I went forward to speak, murmuring from the pews stopped me almost at once. Then, from the back, a sharp rebuke rang out.

"*Tuitui!*" Be silent! It was Tepia a Tevu, Turtle Eggs.

I was as shocked as on the day I had heard Kirov was dead and the terror unleashed. Though, for all that it was, it should not have been surprise. We had all known it would come to that: mass arrests, dissolution of the underground, flight. As now I knew what I had not permitted myself to acknowledge before: the policeman of the atoll was my ally, had been from the first.

"People of Atu-Hiva," I said. "I have come to tell you that from tomorrow socialism will prevail on this isle. No more shall you be poor and fear the white. At dawn tomorrow each male head of family will report to the house of the chief for instruction and work—" A buzz interrupted this, and I paused to turn to my left, where Seventh Man sat trying to contain his surprise. I had debated within myself whether to alert him or not, but I thought he might refuse. By storm I hoped to turn burden to honor. Tepia a Tevu had by now marched to the front and stood beneath the cross, glaring into the pews as I continued.

"Any male head of family who does not go to the house of the chief at dawn shall be sent away from Atu-Hiva in an outrigger and may never return. His possessions will be taken from him. Neither may his children accompany him"—this last was the worst, for the Marquesan loves his family more than his life—"and if he does return he will be killed." I watched the women look to their husbands in fear. "These are the wishes of Tranck Tane. If the people of Atu-Hiva are good, and work well, then they will be rewarded with many presents, free at the store. If not, they will receive no free presents and will starve." There was no murmuring now. A hand touched my sleeve.

It was William Lloyd. His partner stood stiffly at his side. "Captain Zabrodny," the missionary whispered, "This is a house of God."

"Both of you have two weeks to pack your things," I said. "The mail steamer will take you to Ha-o."

The missionary directed my gaze to the near wall, where that original letter from *Monsieur l'Inspecteur des Établissements Français de l'Océanie*, a ragged thing by then, was tacked.

I am certain none of the Marquesans had ever before heard a pistol shot, not at this range. By the time I had holed the *permis* three times the church was empty but for the two missionaries, a stiff Turtle Eggs, and Seventh Man, whose remembered dignity and new-found place would permit no display of fear. At Peace clutched my arm, such indescribable lust in her green eyes that at once I shared it and felt ill.

The remainder of that day I spent in consultation with Goetz, who long before had been advised his book-keeping might be changed. For him it was hardly more than that. Where previously he was paid in copra processed from the nuts fallen from Tranck's trees, now he would be paid through me. We worked out a simple minimum wage in tinned food, flour, sugar and cloth that he would issue free. Left to his discretion this way it was certain the trader would put a bit more aside for his eventual return to Hamburg. He was pleased.

Walking back I took the long route along the beach, peering into the water of the lagoon as though into some future whose end was clear. When I entered the little hut I shared with At Peace, I found inside the old chief. As I had looked into those waters, so did he now look across to the new demi-john. But for the occasional drops of native production he might have sampled over the years, here was more alcohol in one place than the atoll had seen. Turtle Eggs kept a nest of spies—nothing large as this could have been made, or drunk.

"As a sinner I look upon it," Seventh Man said. "Not as a Malachite. As a Malachite, I do not drink."

"The Malachites will soon be gone," I said. From the lean-to kitchen outside, I could smell the baking fish At Peace had earlier speared. "The missionaries have given you nothing but reason to be content with this world in favor of the next. Do you believe in a next world, Seventh Man?"

"As a Malachite or as a man?" His eyes were fixed on the demi-john.

I broke the seal, poured out three cups. "Tranck Tane has told me to put all trust in you, Seventh Man." I watched him empty his cup and set it down to be refilled. "Tranck Tane asks only that you help to bring in a great deal of copra, many nuts, and well-cured, and lead the divers later on when there will be pearl. And for this we will help you again to lead your people."

"They are not mine," he said. "In the old days perhaps, but in the old days we ate our enemies. Now we eat pig." He laughed into the rum. "When there is that. In the old days we dove for pearl. Now we sit in the shade. In the old days we would take from the whites what they had, and if they would not give it, kill. Now we go to the trader and watch him mark his book and know that Tranck Tane pays for what we do not earn."

"That will stop."

"The people will starve."

"The people will produce more," I said. "They will tend the groves and produce only copra of the highest grade. They will no longer be permitted to dry the fruit of green nuts, which spoils."

"The people know it spoils, *pupinay* captain. Should they care if Goetz does not?"

"In the past Goetz was permitted to take whatever was brought. Now he may not. Only good copra will pass. You will inspect it, Seventh Man."

"I?"

"And you will pay those who work."

"I have nothing for them." He finished off the second cup.

"You shall tell Goetz if anyone among the people does not work, then he will not give them goods."

Seventh Man seemed to be weighing something in his mind. "Then what shall come to me?"

As a Malachite or as a sinner, I would have liked to ask. But a bulky shadow had abruptly imposed itself between doorway and declining sun. The room was all but dark.

It was Turtle Eggs. "Tranck Tane has forbidden drink," he said. "Tranck Tane has forbidden it to all."

With the slow dignity of the easily drunk, Seventh Man poured himself a third cup. "I am not all," he said, "I am chief. My father was chief, and his."

"It makes the divers mad," Turtle Eggs said.

"Divers!" Seventh Man laughed. "There is no diving here. There are no pearls. There is nothing, though I too remember the times when we brought up great shells and received many *francs*. But now . . . . Drink you, too, Tepia a Tevu. You and I rule for the *pupinay* captain now. Drink with your chief and this *perofeta* of *Marax*, who has come to free us from the white."

If I did not blush, I should have. For neither was I prophet, still was I white. But I had gone too far not to go on. From inside my belt I withdrew the Nagan pistol which had been my last solid link to what was, and beckoned to the gross policeman of the atoll. "Come and drink," I said. "And have this. It does not befit a socialist to walk about with a stick."

From there on the way was clear. I told them of the years ahead—an Atu-Hivan Five-Year Plan, as Tranck had set it down—and spoke of the wealth to be earned from the culture of pearl compared to what could be wrought from the declining market in copra. I promised that if we seeded the lagoon that year, within another five these waters, which had brought forth only the occasional prize, would provide a harvest. If Mikimoto could do it in Japan, producing almost perfect specimens in many hues, we could as well. And where his oysters were at best four inches wide, the Marquesan, *margaritifera maxima*, is commonly three times the size. I had seen enough of Tranck's Tahitian experiments to know we would succeed, but this very certainty counterposed a doubt within my own heart. Those who knew better had sent me here not for all time.

But if they no longer lived? I was to discover later that the situation of the democratic opposition in the Soviet Union was far worse than even my worst imaginings. Perhaps my place was, indeed, now here. Though the Marquesan was ready to do as he had been told, I still had choice. But that night, this door so clearly opened, as abruptly closed. While At Peace and I lay back upon our pallet and listened to the soft thumps of ripe coconuts falling from their heights, she confided in me with a girl's quaint pride. She was with child.

The past again intervened. In its light, the future lay exposed. What had I done to the people of this atoll I had not known to exist the year before? What had I done to this woman I could not love?

*

By nature the Russian has never been able to see clearly. It astounds me now that I could not have predicted the energy and pride the Atu-Hivans threw into their work. Island peoples had never been able to rely on others for aid, and these Marquesans, who had lived unnaturally upon charity, began with a vengeance to take their lives into their own hands.

Almost at once the coconut plantations were cleared of rubbish and volunteer growth, older poorly bearing trees removed. At the beach, a central copra-drying point and packing shed was built. I had spoken to Seventh Man of industrial specialization, but I'd had no idea this would supply the ideology, ready-made, for a return to the old ways. A system of *tapu* began slowly to re-emerge: the copra-dryers were no longer permitted to pick up the fallen ripe nuts or tend to the trees; the agriculturists no long dried copra on their own. At last the cutter was repaired—as it could have been many months before—by a ship's carpenter, trained at Papeete, who had spent his Atu-Hivan years playing dominos in the shade. A fishing fleet of outriggers was organized with each morning's catch drawn up on the beach for the women to pick through, though any female who touched a fish still in the canoe was reprimanded by the leaders of the fleet. Long before, it had been forbidden for a woman to lay hands upon a canoe. Now, the old *tapu* was revived. Perhaps because of these half-remembered traditions, there was none of the griping attendant to centrally organized work as I had seen it in Moscow or Leningrad. Seventh Man seemed instinctively to know the right thing, though when he released to the women Goetz's entire stock of cloth—the trader did not mind: he took his profit on each inch—I feared they would make *pareus* and forsake all else. But I was wrong, as I had been in thinking that by example I could make socialists of anyone. By their own example, the Atu-Hivans made a socialist of me.

The women turned all their cloth into *pareus*, yes. But these disappeared into the cutter, which set out for

Ha-o to trade, bringing back none of the useless trinkets I would have expected, but metal fishhooks, timber, nails, and a dozen banana stalks. I may have doubted that bananas could be grown in coral sand, but I could not doubt the ingenuity of these people I had all but despised for not understanding them at all. No manual had been printed, no instructions called out. But these Atu-Hivans, dregs of the capitalist society which had been imposed upon their own, were now making a society again. Turtle Eggs, the very symbol of that disease the foreigners had brought, now turned to training a militia armed with shell-tipped spears, which patrolled the lagoon beach as though at any moment General Denekin's White Guards might be expected to appear. A French gunboat arrived instead, anchoring beyond the outer reef. But for only a moment was I permitted to fear.

Seventh Man promptly assembled the militia at attention before Goetz's store, Turtle Eggs proudly to the fore wearing my pistol like a badge, and called out all the people to sing the *Marseillaise* as the French captain stepped ashore, followed by the two Malachite missionaries of a barely remembered past. If the singing did not bring tears to the young officer's eyes, it did to mine. In my youth, even more than the *Internationale*, this was the socialist's hymn. Seventh Man kissed the Frenchman on each cheek, but he need not have whispered when he said, "*Nous les ne voulons pas! N'acceptons pas des relations bizarres sur l'isle!*" I doubt the missionaries understood. They were still protesting when the red-faced captain shooed them back into the ship's boat, each clutching his black hat.

Only Goetz was not amused. This was in keeping with his sourness of the months past. He was making more money than ever, but it was not until the night before Tranck himself arrived that I understood.

The trader was drunk, and while the women ate separately on the terrace—according to Marquesan custom, which no insult attends—I found myself, as usual, listening more than I spoke. I was his guest and, more than that, knew he was right: Tranck was surely coming out to give him the sack. A trader was hardly necessary now. The German would be left at an unpleasant crossing. He had come to the Marquesas to make his fortune. Having failed, he must either go out to some further atoll and again set up store, or return to Hamburg in defeat. Thus, with each bottle of Patzenhoffer his hatred grew, though I shall never believe he was, by essence, bad. It was merely that he had nothing of faith or the grace of having participated in something greater than himself. Yet he did have something I did not, for he was able to look the future in the eye and see some prospect at least, where all I saw was the past writ large. I had not heard from my family in so long that each time the mail steamer dropped anchor beyond the outer reef I had to force myself to paddle out. It had become an unendurable ceremony of pain: what had become of my family, of the Russia that I loved? But Goetz never looked back. His future was rosy enough, if only his personal devil could be dead.

"Tranck!" he said, as though pronouncing a curse. "We are all Tranck's, Captain Zabrodny. All of us. I, you, *monsieur le chef.* When the white men in these seas are relegated to clerk . . .Do you know Seventh Man sends his deputies now to order from the store. I'll not work for a *kanaque*, not yet . . ."

"You work for Tranck, Herr Goetz."

"The Trancks of this world . . ." He leaned across the table. A beer bottle clanked to the coral floor. "Making deals over our bodies, Captain Zabrodny. Tell me, why should men such as we be ruled by the Trancks . . .by those who are keeping us down, captain?" He was whispering now, staring into my eyes searchingly. "A new order, captain, in which . . .in which . . ."

"From new orders many have suffered, Herr Goetz."

"They must! Races and races, captain. You and I, look at us, blond, strong . . ."

But Goetz was hardly blond, and I felt weak as never before. It was neither climate nor disease, but a simple longing for home. "Yes, yes," I said, mocking him gently and myself not enough. "You speak now to just that thing, the product of such a new order in the flesh—Soviet man."

This mild jest seemed to throw him into a rage. He stood, sneering into the cool night. "Soviet man?" His laugh was more than a drunk's, and less. "What I will take from these islands is a start in my fatherland, captain, where a true new order is being made, based on something greater than fear. But you—what will you? Your tattooed pleasure-giver, what will she be put to in your Soviet state? Building bridges, paving roads? She will die there in the cold, but not only this. The months before her death of longing for these skies, these seas, will be not her punishment but yours. Who are you—who is Tranck!— to meddle in God's plan? These savages will never be men, and neither will they be savages again. Take one look at them, at ourselves . . ."

At this I was prepared to leave, but as with many drunks, a sudden, stormy clarity took hold of the German. He gripped my sleeve and drew me close. "Wait!" And so I stood, barely hearing him stumbling against the crude furniture while a final bit of the past descended upon me, as though something in the night had shaken it loose. And for a moment I was present in both worlds: one in which the trader Goetz bumped about in an adjoining room as outside two Marquesan women, their meal long done, embroidered baby blankets by the light of a moon which eclipsed the Southern Cross, and at the very same time I was in another world, where I stood with a dark-haired woman in a disused room at an official function, a formal party of the Commercial Academy in Nikolsky Street, close by the Kremlin walls. We stood very close, I remember. "With me there is no need for evasion," she said.

I was seized with longing, and with dread. It was the 5th of November, 1932. In a few days, I would be following her coffin to the frozen patch that would be her inheritance, a simple Novodevichy grave. I shuddered with hopelessness. "But you are...."

"I am Nadezhda Alleluyeva," she said, breathing softly. "Not your secretary-general."

Beside myself, I took her in my arms, kissed her—once. A sudden noise from the party outside had violated our private room, and when I shook myself free of her I realized I was no longer in two places but in one. And the drunken trader, Wilhelm Goetz, was gripping my shoulder, while his other hand held a stack of letters tied with string. I knew them at once, and knew as well why in all the months I had been at Atu-Hiva I had had not one reply.

✳

Tranck's arrival in the schooner the next afternoon was cause for general celebration, and Seventh Man was careful to orchestrate this so that everything accomplished in the months of Tranck's absence was shown at its best. The cutter had gone out to the outer reef to take Tranck off, and by the time it was tied up at the narrow quay the entire population of Atu-Hiva was on the beach. The *Marseil-laise* was sung again, and then the traditional melodies of the *himene*. The old man went among the population distributing gifts, shaking hands, kissing the women and tossing their children high into the air. My letters to him had erred only in understating the changes in the atoll, but he must have had reports from Goetz, and knew that the old Atu-Hiva was no more. Now there was not the tiniest child who did not receive his prize: a knife of tin for the boys, ribbons for the girls, needles and thread for the women and shiny lead-pencils for the men, though only their chief could write. Seventh Man was visibly satisfied with what he had wrought. I kept to the background with At Peace, her belly swollen, to leave the chief his full measure of pride.

If I had once envied Tranck his knowledge of those times when the Marquesans were truly men, I felt no envy now. How proud Lenin must have been! Yes, but with that thought came the ever corresponding blow, for Lenin's rule had passed, and I knew enough of the course of events to know that on this balmy atoll this same smiling Seventh Man would one night have too much of drink and begin to suspect some treason previously unknown. Or would it be Turtle Eggs who would turn the spear-armed guard against his chief? For one who lived so much in the past, this future was enough clear, though for the moment only gladness reigned. Seventh Man declared a feast.

While preparations were being made, Tranck sat within our house and gazed into his daughter's eyes, speaking of the child. He had too long desired a grandson for his old age. Me, he treated like a son—unloading a fresh white-linen suit in my size, a case of Russian books he had taken the trouble to acquire, another demi-john.

He was most interested in our progress with the pearls, and nodded when I outlined, as we walked along the lagoon, where the markers would be placed, where the shell set out. I mentioned Goetz.

"A trader, my kind," he said, and waved his hand. "Buyin' and sellin', marchin' to no drumbeat but the slap of *francs*."

"You'll send him away, I suppose."

Tranck laughed. "'Twasn't for the likes of Goetz I made this place, but for At Peace and her man."

"I do care for her, Tranck."

"'Twas my intent," he said, laughing again. "Have her then, and with it the atoll. Ah, what a start! Atu-Hiva's a mere spark, but a spark's a beacon where there's darkness all about. Comrade Stalin would be proud."

"To hell with Comrade Stalin, Tranck." I said it softly as I could. "He's a butcher. You know it as well as I. No Wall Street tyrant could behave as he. The best of the Soviet Union are dead or in chains." I stopped. The sun was going down fast, the lagoon submerged in its own reflected light of purple and gold. Idly I wondered how I had managed to make of this beauty a commonplace. I would it miss it now. "All Russia is in chains, Tranck."

"'Tis the world's in chains," he said, calm as the surface of the lagoon. "The thing's to make it better; work from within. Make the best of what is."

"Is this, then, making the best?" I withdrew from my pocket the stack of letters I had gotten from Goetz. "Unopened, Tranck. Unmailed. Unread. As Soviet postman, your servant Goetz would have made a fine career." I dropped them at his feet. "Would you be Stalin too?"

He sighed. Even now I have no reason to believe it signified anything other than the full measure of the sadness he felt for me, for himself. "The world's comin' apart, Grisha," he said. "The smell of war, 'tis all about, though you may not know it in this place. But 'twill come. 'Twill come to Moscow and Paris and Tahiti and New York—wherever there be civilized men. The English scum conquered by the German dross, the Jap to stab the Dutch, the Yank . . ." But he left off. "Chaos, lad. 'Twill be chaos everywhere—but here. Atu-Hiva will be safe, Grisha. It's a dot, not worth a damn to anyone but you and me. We can make somethin' here, lad, some sense in a world that . . ." His voice trailed off, then as suddenly rose. "Listen to me, lad! I brought my daughter to this place to be raised among her kind. I feared for her in Papeete. War will come to Papeete, Grisha. 'Twill swirl about these islands. But with luck, with the luck I had when first I came jumpin' out of that poisonous galley as I did, you and At Peace might live here to old age, in dignity, and make your people prosper and be proud. This lagoon, well-managed, will return a harvest in pearl to buy whatever cannot be grown. A modest yield will be worth its weight in thousand-*franc* notes. Here our people can survive, Grisha, safe and well."

"They are not our people, Tranck. Not yours, not mine."

"At Peace is my daughter, as are you your own mother's son!"

"She is Marquesan, the last of what was."

"By half, only by half."

"By half or whole, Tranck, I do care for her, don't you see? In my own way I love her as you must have loved her mother when you hid by Fautaua Falls, as we love this atoll, this dream . . ."

"Then have her, lad. Please. With vows or not, have her and make children by her and raise them as you would. This place can flourish—you've seen that. Make it the place your own cannot be."

"It can," I said.

"'Tisn't now."

"It isn't now," I was forced to agree.

That long night I sat through a feast in Tranck's honor, and in mine. But the next morning with Tranck I sailed. From the taffrail of the schooner we waved to At Peace, and she to us. As many men have murmured in these climes, I promised to return. I told her I was merely off to war—the defense of my native land—though we both knew my words were meant to conceal the wound, not heal it. And when I explained to her that I had been saved from Stalin's fury to preserve him from the Germans' wrath, neither to me did it make any sense at all. Even in the turbulence of the years ahead, it would be sordid and a lie. Why is it, I asked myself, when we are so close to what we wish for, we must turn? For At Peace I had seen no life amid my native snows, and for me none at all in paradise.

Based on a
True Story

Video meliora proboque detiora sequor.
Seeing the better I acknowledge it, but follow the worse.
—Ovid

Though Racetrack Films was small compared to the Big Five, and had never even come close to so much as an Oscar nomination since the first Academy Awards were presented ten years before, EZ Shelupsky ran his lot like a smaller, sepia version of the majors. MGM had dozens of sound stages and thousands of employees, including a cast of contract players whose faces were known even in the smallest towns around the world; Shelupsky had only one sound stage, at that about as small as a high-school cafeteria, and he employed fewer than a dozen full-timers. But he did control the screens in some five hundred colored movie houses, and his featured players—Deidre Lucky, Earl Mayson, Lucy Moses, Grant Lincoln and Delila Waters— were as well known to Negro America as MGM's Mickey Rooney and Judy Garland or Universal's Deanna Durbin and WC Fields were on the white side of the color line. The Big Five shared an enormous market, but Racetrack Films was sole proprietor of its own special piece of real estate. That year, 1939—often considered Hollywood's best year ever—when the majors were releasing *Beau Geste, Babes in*

Arms, Confessions of a Nazi Spy, The Wizard of Oz, Mr. Smith Goes to Washington, to say nothing of *Gone With the Wind*, EZ Shelupsky was cranking out *The Brown Buckaroo, Curse of the Colored Mummy* and *Holiday in Harlem*—and making more money on every dollar invested.

For what it's worth, EZ could never have done it without me, or—to inject a note of modesty that is alien to Hollywood—someone very like me.

Not that a white writer would have had all that much trouble creating the plots of these pictures, which were about as original as most B-movies of the time, but the dialogue, the dark wit, the pizzazz was something a white man could not be expected to fake. Shelupsky knew enough about his audience to know that colored slang reinvented itself about every other week, that how Negroes danced and sang and played music was as changeable as the weather—Southern California excepted—and that the concerns of Afro-Americans were so different from those of the majority population they might have been another nationality. Maybe EZ was a little jealous of the majors—producing what were called race movies would certainly get you a table up front in the Plantation Club in that part of Los Angeles that white folks called "The Jungle;" it was not going to get you invited to the White House—but he knew what he had.

"Them, they got three thousand theaters to split between five studios; me, I got, on my own, five hundred houses. Let me explain you the math. When you're adding it all up and dividing, they got six hundred apiece, sometimes, not all the time, because it flows and ebbs. I'll give you a hint. It's not just the screens. When you do the addition, don't forget to carry the popcorn, the candy, the cigarettes, in some places the booze they sell in the lobby, out of all of which I get a piece. Now let me put in some algebra.

Them, they got people spend a quarter every time they go to the movies? Me, I got people only spend a dime—hey, okay, your average colored theater is no Loew's Alhambra—but my people, God bless 'em, they spend their dime three, four, maybe five times a week. Why? Because my films are so mysterious they got to watch them over and over to find out the secret? Pretty to think so, but the real reason is simple. Colored people got nothing else to spend on. They don't own big houses, most can't afford cars—yeah, sure people make jokes about coons in Cadillacs, but how many Cadillacs you see and how many Negroes driving them that they ain't the chauffeur? Even if they could afford it, they can't get into expensive restaurants. Hattie McDaniel, a featured player in white movies for twelve years—she just won an Oscar, first and last time that's going to happen for a long while—they won't let her in half the night clubs in this town, and the other half don't usually see a lot of blue eyes. What I got is a franchise, a country inside a country. You know what, when I see injustice, mistreatment of colored people, sometimes out-and-out crime against them, as a human being I'm angry, but as a business man, a producer, as soon as they let the colored into white movie theaters I'm a dead corpse. There goes my franchise, *foof*. You might say I'm a split-up personality—half of me wants them to have the rights they should, the other says: Keep 'em down a year longer. I got costs."

Say what you will about EZ Shelupsky, and in today's climate he is sometimes depicted as a kind of Hollywood Simon Legree, a son of a bitch—nobody ever called him anything less than shrewd: the *next* black actor to win an Oscar was Sidney Poitier, thirty-five years later—he was an equal opportunity son of a bitch. White, colored, Japanese, Mexican, he made everyone wait, made everyone nervous, made all kinds of people rich and all kinds of people miserable. He made me happy almost as often as he made me want to crawl under a rock and die, but whatever his effect on you it had little to do with race in a business where black-and-white was not simply what came before Technicolor. In a town where in 1938 the Los Angeles branch of the NAACP petitioned the Hays Office, the industry's self-appointed regulator, to demand roles for Negroes that weren't maids, doormen or railroad porters (yours truly helped frame the petition, though it didn't do much: *Gone With the Wind* opened the next year with the mama of all colored maids), in Shelupsky's films colored people played doctors, lawyers, cops, cowboys, desperados, businessmen, secretaries, farmers, teachers, ministers, even politicians. It was so rare to find a pale face in a Shelupsky film, the credits used to include "Joe Smith (or whatever the name). . . White Man." As EZ liked to say, "At Racetrack, even the horses are colored." Most of the people on his payroll, starting with Alma, his secretary for 12 years, were Negroes, and they got treated as badly as any secretary, casting director or writer in Hollywood, white, black or indifferent. If you could get in to see him, that is.

Aside from his bookie, his barber and his tailor, no one even got on the lot to see EZ Shelupsky unless Alma gave them a four-digit code number which had to match one of the numbers she left at the gate every morning. Shelupsky hardly needed to have his secretary go this far—leaving just a name at the gate would do—but even for a studio head Shelupsky was known for a stubborn megalomania; unlike the others, this was rivaled by a kind of pig-headed magnanimity. Though he didn't have to, he paid his players pretty much what B-movie white actors

got, and treated them with an off-hand respect that confused them as much as it pleased.

A bundle of prickly contradictions, Shelupsky had
in his decade in Hollywood created so many legends that
the jokesters at Chasen's practically choked over their Beef
Belmont (braised short ribs and matzah balls—Hollywood
on a plate) and claimed he had Alma write his personality quirks out on index cards so he could remember them
all; less pleasantly, they claimed he had his *shvartze* actors
wear name tags because they all looked alike. One thing
about EZ: no one looked like *him*.

The other Jewish studio heads had sharp Eastern
European features, distinct noses, jutting chins, chiseled
eye sockets, even sculpted ears, but everything about EZ
was rounded; though his 5-foot-8-inch frame didn't carry
an ounce of fat, he seemed to be composed of a complete
set of fully integrated knobs. After the war I played tennis
with him regularly, and he was all muscle, but even this was
rounded, as though he had been stuffed with tennis balls
in his arms and softballs in his legs; his shoulders were like
volleyballs. When he pursed his thin lips in concentration,
it was as if his chin and nose had decided to mate—they
were that congruent. His hair was prematurely gray and
thinning on top; he kept it short, which further rounded
him off. If he'd worn anything but the best custom-made
suits he might have looked like a stack of bowling balls,
but the elegance of his dress, always in an unexpected color
or an unusual stripe or windowpane check set off by a brilliant white shirt, gave him a smooth, unflappable look.
He was hardly unflappable. Too many writers and directors
and moviehouse owners had seen him in full flap.

From everyone else he demanded consistency,
particularly in grooming ("Maybe you can't tell a book by

the cover"—this from a man who admitted he had never read one—"but it's a good start") and the ability to turn crap into cash ("You know why Hamlet don't make a movie? Not enough tap dancing"), but when it came to himself he insisted only on the kind of radical contradiction that defied expectation, keeping his colleagues and employees perpetually off-balance and amusing the studio boss no end. A staunch capitalist, Shelupsky was nevertheless a student not of Dale Carnegie, whose *How to Make Friends and Influence People* became a bestseller in '37 and stayed popular into the 50s, but of Joseph Stalin, EZ having recognized in the Soviet dictator the focused ability to scare the *bupkes* out of anyone who so much as heard his name. Of course Stalin did not share Shelupsky's signal weakness.

When he had first come out to the coast Shelupsky visited Santa Anita almost every day. For the 1937 Kentucky Derby, in which EZ had a horse, he'd had a dedicated phone line installed on his desk, directly connected to Churchill Downs where War Admiral had, unfortunately, won. The other studio heads liked horses—Shelupsky loved them. As a boy in Poland he had used to ride Friesians, big plow horses with hooves as big as his head—"A regular *sheigetz,* they called me!"—but when he came to an urbanized America he'd had to give this up until he became rich enough to own thoroughbreds. Only one thing was wrong. They—the blueblood trustees of the Turf Club that ran Santa Anita—would not let an EZ Shelupsky in as a member. It wasn't personal. He could run horses there, he could practically live in the clubhouse, he could throw his money around and hire the best trainers and jocks, but at membership a line was drawn. Once they let the Shelupskys in, they might as well let in the Japs and the greasers and the shines. In EZ's words, "They anti-semitted me out."

Which is why Shelupsky and Jack Warner and the other studio heads, along with a few featured players like George Jessel and Al Jolson, and several of the bigger agents, started Hollywood Park—it was the Jewish track. "Fuck the goyim," was so much the Shelupsky motto it might as well have been emblazoned on his jockeys' silks. In fact it was: his horses ran under the blue and green colors of FTG Stables.

Paradoxically, his feeling for the other half of the gentile species was altogether different. "*Shiksas* got refinement," he would say to his casting directors, as though there was a chance in hell they might mistakenly cast a colored Jewess. "Let the other guy have a million Fanny Brices— give me a Claudette Colbert every time. Your high-class *shiksa* she don't even shit. Maybe pees a little." In 1936 he divorced his first wife, who apparently was too often in the powder room engaging in smelly Hebraic physicality, and took up with the platinum-haired princess of Hollywood, Nora Bright. Not only was she no semite, but she loved horseflesh, loved the track, loved betting, and just adored being Mrs. EZ Shelupsky. For one thing, the roles got better—every studio head in Hollywood was her husband's best friend. For another, EZ worked so hard he bothered her for sex only once a week—it wasn't that she didn't like action, but her tastes, it turned out, were identical to her husband's: along with the ponies, she had a fondness for the ladies. Either way, she would have understood: EZ was tired at night for good reason. He gave at the office. And on the set. Sometimes in his marvelously capacious Brewster towncar on the way to the track. But never *there*. Horse racing was his religion. EZ avoided synagogues. His temple was the track.

In the depths of the depression, Shelupsky's horses ate better than 99% of the American people, and he spent more on his ponies on any given day than was needed for a month's care and feeding of the average American family. By 1939 FTG Stables carried forty-eight thoroughbreds, and his trainer was none other than Ozzie Hirsch, whose horse had almost beat out War Admiral in the Derby. Though Ozzie would train a pot-bellied pig if an owner required it, Hirsch liked leggy, short-coupled horses with tight conformation and good manners, which was pretty much EZ's taste in actresses, one of which—a striking octoroon with an aggressive set to her chin; like so many of the new wave of actresses, if you cut her hair and taped her breasts she could pass, á la Marlene Dietrich, for her own leading man—was just leaving when Alma buzzed me in. "Mr. S, Laurence Bellringer coming through."

"EZ!" I said, as though I had not seen him for a long time. It had been five weeks, a century in Hollywood. Shelupsky did that to people. If you were working on a script, you would see him three times a day and get phoned five times in the middle of the night, but as soon as you were off payroll you became a stranger. I found myself pumping the studio head's meaty hand like a well handle in Botke, the Polish village of Shelupsky's youth that the mogul talked about sometimes when he was in the mood. "You look *so* good."

"You got five minutes, Larry. You wanna kiss my ass with it, be my guest." Shelupsky examined his Gerard-Perigaux. "Nu?"

"The year is 1654—"

"Where?"

"New York."

"They had a New York in sixteen-something?"

"Nieuw Amsterdam, you're right," I said, having learned early that any piece of information a third-grader might be expected to know had to be passed along in a tone of voice that was as much complicitous as informative—*of course* you know this, EZ, *of course* you know that. "Of course you know the Dutch are in charge, EZ, and the mayor, what they called the *burgomeister*—of course you know that—is the famous one-legged Peter Stuyvesant, a real sneaky bastard—think Charles Laughton, but premenstrual. First line of the movie: 'I want this scum off my island!'"

"What island?"

"Manhattan."

"What scum?"

"Ah," I whispered dramatically. "I got you at *scum.* The fourth word in the movie and I got you."

"What you got is four *minutes.*"

"The scum in question is on a boat, the St. Cathriene, which is jam-packed with . . ."

Shelupsky rolled his eyes. "Less than four minutes and you're playing acting school? Just give it to me, what's on the boat? Coconuts? Booze? The Harlem Globetrotters?" Suddenly he had a thought. "Chorus girls?"

"None of the above, EZ. What's on the boat is . . ."

"Either tell me what's on the boat or get the fuck personally out of my office, Bellringer."

I allowed my voice to drop an octave. I had taken a risk. Now was the pay-off. "What's . . .on . . .the . . .boat . . .is . . ."

"*Wha-at?*"

I spelled it out. "J-E-W-S."

Shelupsky's office suddenly became so quiet you could hear a featured player's contract being torn up on the floor below. The studio head looked at his watch, platinum and gold, a gift from Nora, after all. Slowly he raised his eyes. "What?"

"Jews."

"What Jews?"

"Jews," I said. "Jews, like . . . Jews."

"What Jews? Colored Jews? You want I should make a movie about colored Jews? Larry, sometimes I think you got shtupped so much in the rear end it made your brains fluffy. My young friend, Racetrack don't make movies about Jews. Despite what they think at the Turf Club—and those fucking cock-sucker *goyim*, no offense, should go intercourse themselves—Jews are white people. Racetrack don't make movies about white people. Racetrack makes movies about coloreds. Jesse Lasky makes movies about white people, Sammy Goldwyn makes movies about white people, everybody else makes movies about white people. EZ Shelupsky makes movies about *not* white people. That's why I got you to write for me. If I was so stupid to make movies about white people you'd be out of a job. Because what you know about white people you could write in a homo picture book. Anyway, even the regular studios don't make movies about Jews."

"That's exactly right, EZ."

"Exactly right is not an argument, Larry. If you're agreeing with me, we're not having a discussion. In other words, we don't need other words. Larry, what are you trying to say, that you want me to get out of the colored movie business and go into the Jewish movie business?"

"No, sir. Race films are a good business, and as far as I can see they're good for my people."

"Damned straight. They give colored people hope, dignity, a sense of who they are. You think I'm in this for the money? I'm sure you do, and you're not wrong. It's a business. But so's poetry. You know what's the motto of MGM? *Ars Gratia Artis*. It's on all their pictures. Means "art for the sake of art." Louie Mayer told me when he stuck it on his movies he didn't even know if it meant anything. And you know what? It don't. Without art being a business, it wouldn't be fly-paper on a wall. You think Rembrandt painted for the pleasure? It was his racket. He got paid for it. Also Beethoven with piano playing. Also . . ." Here the studio head seemed to run out of famous artist-entrepreneurs. He tried another tack. "You know the letters we get from colored people thanking us for giving them movies of their own? Without Racetrack Films, Larry, the American Negro would be invisible, even to himself. So what's with you and Jewish movies? Is this a joke or what?"

"You know as well as I do, EZ, that colored films don't have a future."

The studio head looked at me like I had questioned the sanctity of democracy, or capitalism, or horse racing. "I know no such a thing."

"Then you're not as smart as I think you are, EZ. As everyone thinks you are."

EZ's mouth twisted up like a deftly peeled lemon rind. "Okay, I'm listening."

"We're going to have a war."

"Maybe," Shelupsky said. "Probably. If it isn't on Roosevelt's mind, even though he keeps denying, it's on that bastard Hitler's. Eventually. Yeah, I agree. So?"

"So people like me are going to be in the service, and certain barriers are going to fall."

"As much as I'd like to think so, Larry, I'm not sure. I'm sure they got homos in the Navy, but that's the Navy. It's the tight pants."

"Not homos, EZ."

"Harvard men?" Shelupsky was much impressed with the fact that though I was more educated than he, he was the one who signed the checks. "Or is that the same as homos?"

I wonder which he thought was worse. "Neither homos nor Harvard men, EZ. Negroes."

"From your mouth to Roosevelt's ear. But to tell you the truth, I doubt it."

"Even now, theaters in the North are dissolving the color line. In New York there's no such thing as colored-only houses. Maybe a few in Harlem, but that's just geography. Dark people are going to light people's shows, but light people aren't going to dark people's."

"New York ain't America."

"San Francisco? Chicago? Detroit?" I said. "You know that it's happening all over. Even in L.A."

"Two-thirds of this country is in little towns where the mayor can't read and the whole city council is spelled K.K.K. That's the America you're *not* looking at. All of life isn't a big city."

"Things are going to be changing, EZ. You don't want to hang your hat on something that's not going to be there when you want to put it back on your head."

Oddly, perhaps because it seemed to echo Shelupsky's own inconsistent syntax, this thought seemed to strike home. He looked at me for a moment like an equal. No, not regarding race. I would never know what was in the studio head's heart regarding the colored question. But as a movie man.

"You trying to tell me something, Bellringer?"

"Yes, sir."

"That I'm in a dying business?"

"It's got some life in it, but not a lot."

"It's always darkest before the storm," Shelupsky said.

There was no sense in correcting him, especially when he was right. "So we should branch out," I said.

"We?"

"If I'm right, we. If I'm not, not."

"You're offering me a partnership in my own company? Is that what you're saying?"

"Is that too uppity for you, EZ?"

Shelupsky did not like being on the wrong end of the racial stick. He was a big contributor to Negro colleges, Negro hospitals, everything Negro but the NAACP, which to EZ's mind was just another way to say "Commie." That year we had sent a delegation to the World Conference Against Hate in Moscow. "I think you're a disgusting cock-sucking, homosexual faggot, Larry. But as a colored man, I don't condemn you. You were born the way you are."

"I was also born a disgusting, cock-sucking, homosexual faggot, EZ."

"You mean to say that kind of thing ain't a matter of choice?"

"Is this about who I fuck or movies about Jews?"

"Neither," he said. "You know I don't care about your personal life. You're a terrific writer. An artist. Even Michelangelo, I heard this somewhere, was queer as a lead penny. Most painters, in fact. It's an artistic disease. If God was to strike dead every poof in Hollywood, we'd be down to one feature a year and it would be terrible. But your idea that Racetrack should make Jewish films, that's…"

"Laughable," I said. "Like what, talkies?" This was a low blow. Shelupsky had been late making the transition from silents. He was sensitive about it. He saw himself as an innovator, but he had missed that one. "Start a new company. No relation to Racetrack. There's a lot of talent here. Jewish talent."

"The refugees? Larry, they don't even talk English."

"Billy Wilder?"

"A exception."

"Joseph von Sternberg?"

"Two apples don't make a fig tree."

"I'll write the dialogue. We'll get the refugees for story, for structure. The whole German movie industry is here, and they're all Jews."

"Yeah, but that doesn't mean they should write movies for Jews. Let them write for everybody, like the rest of the industry. You know how many Jews there are in America? Two percent of the population. I looked it up."

"You're doing pretty well with ten percent of the population, and most Negroes don't have two nickels to rub together. And don't forget Europe. That's sixteen million more Jews, at least." I allowed myself the luxury of a wink. "I looked it up."

"Jews go to movies? Who knows if they do?"

"You think they don't?"

"Yeah, they probably do."

"A couple or three titles a year, something big that other people will go see as well. *Gone With the Wind*, but for Jews. Or maybe just about them."

"I got no distribution. What am I going to do, show it in Selma, Alabama? Philadelphia, Mississippi? If it's a picture that's appealing for Jews, then it's got to be shown in houses in Jewish neighborhoods. In L.A., I wouldn't even have distribution in Boyle Heights, the biggest ghetto east of Warsaw. I got three screens in Watts, but I don't got Boyle Heights."

"The Big Five will fight to give you distribution. They're your friends."

"They're my friends because I'm not a competitor. And they'll take half the gross. And *all* the popcorn and candy."

I was waiting for this. Shelupsky's internal adding machine was already computing cash-flow, negotiating gross versus net, figuring angles. That was his job, and I trusted him to do it well. If the deal didn't make money then it wasn't a deal, but there was something I could do to nudge it ahead, like a player at a pinball machine supplying a bit of body-English to drop the steel sphere into the right hole. "With all you've done for the colored people, EZ, don't you think it's time to do something for your own?"

He smiled. "To the Jews I give already plenty. I gave a wing to Cedars of Lebanon. There wouldn't be a Cedars if not for EZ Shelupsky. You can't die of cancer in L.A. without reading the name EZ Shelupsky. Don't make me out a cheapskate for the Jews."

"Anyone can give money, EZ. You can give your talent, your skill, your heart."

"Larry, I thought you was one hell of a writer, for a colored man or even a white man, but now I see you are a topflight bullshit artist also. I take off my hat to you." One beat, two, three. "There was Jews then, in New York?"

"That's when they arrived. In 1654."

"They had immigration? Then?"

"Immigration?"

"Ellis Island."

"No," I managed to get out, forgetting in my excitement with the way the conversation was going that I had to be careful in presenting facts. "Only Peter Stuyvesant. The mayor, the head of the colony. And he didn't like Jews."

"Who does? So what happened?"

"Ah," I began.

"Don't *ah* me—what am I, a ear-nose-and-throat? Do I look like a doctor to you?"

"EZ, you look like a man on the verge of something really big, really—"

"Then hold the *ahs* in your overworked *tuchis* and tell the story. I admit: You got my interest." Shelupsky turned a look on me that probably had been invented by Stalin. "So far."

II

The problem was that in my excitement at having his ear, I ended up telling EZ Shelupsky not one story, but three. More or less I had figured out the central tale, but I was having trouble stitching the plots together: the package eluded me. At $500 per for six weeks, I could write bang-up dialogue—alcohol and the occasional stick of weed helped—but when it came to structure and plot, I was compelled to fall back on the Hollywood concept of character that derived from the patented personality of the actor playing the part: a David Niven type was thus suave, English, polite and selfless, so he never got the girl; an Errol Flynn buckled swash, so he did; a Cary Grant, though born Archie Leach, a lower-class Brit, became the soul of blue-blooded American charm, swinging from debonair to flaky, and would always come through in the end, so his bipolar personality dictated the plot as well. At Racetrack I had my own stable of similarly type-cast stars, practically members of the family to Afro-American moviegoers, but here I was out of my depth: with no actors attached—Racetrack had no stable of white players—I had to invent real characters; with only the rudiments of history, I had to invent a story—and then structure that over a hundred minutes of screen time. However brilliant I was at dialogue, EZ was not paying me $500 a week to learn someone else's job. Enter Fritz von Blum.

Blum may have been his real name—why would anyone make that up?—but I never bought the "von," which seemed of a piece with the shamelessly ersatz nobility of a Mortimer de Rosenne [Marvin Rosen], a Hayward Sigalle [Howard Siegal] or a Clarence LeVigne [Charley Levine]. These producers, talented as they were, managed to undercut their own legitimacy by claiming a pedigree that was clearly wishful, the kind of who-are-you-kidding I was later to witness among my own people when they named their children Percy 23X or Shaquila. Sure, John Garfield had started out in life as Jacob Julius Garfinkle, Kirk Douglas as Isser Danielovitch Demsky, and Sylvia Sydney was born Sophia Kosow, but they were freshly christened according to the demands of a studio system producing movies for an American audience that the studio heads sincerely believed was mono-cultural. Of course it wasn't; Hollywood's Moishe-come-latelies saw only us and them. But why change your name when as a producer or a writer it never appeared on a marquee? *Von* Blum? Unlike his fellow kraut Jo Sternberg, who became Josef von Sternberg in California, Fritz had added on the noble *von* while still in Europe, where he was a mainstay at UFA, the MGM of Germany, having written twenty-two films before Hitler came along and declared the German film industry *juden-rein*. So it was something of a surprise that Fritz's first words to me were, "You know, Mr. Bellringer, I have never before worked with a nigger."

We were in my bungalow at the Garden of Allah, pretty much the only place in L.A. that would accept coloreds—that is, outside of the dark neighborhoods—and for the moment I was confused. Here was this little German twerp wearing clothes that had been out of date in America when they were new, along with bottle-bottom green-tinted spectacles I suspected were pure window glass—you could see his pale eyes through them without distortion. Maybe five-foot-five-inches, probably with elevator shoes, von Blum was of a peculiarly translucent peach complexion, a squashed-in nose, his strawberry hair buzz-cut in a style that would not be popular in America until after the war, and on his left cheek a scar, about an inch-and-a-half long. Aside from that he looked like anyone else who was part European intellectual and, with a head too big for his body, part newt. "You know, Mr. von Blum, we American niggers don't like to be referred to as such. One of those things. Try colored."

"As in the French flag?" he asked.

Because Fritz so far had not so much as cracked the rumor of a smile—now the only clue was the sensation that little lights had been lit behind his eyes—I did not get it. "What?"

"Le tricolore?"

Abruptly I caught on and despite myself, let loose a laugh. Most people in Hollywood would not have called it the tri-color, because to do that one had to speak French, or be familiar with something other than the daily truths the American Communist Party was force-feeding the entire film community, including me. And of course it was a political joke. People did not make *political* jokes in Hollywood in 1939. Anything political was as serious as our films were not. "You're a funny guy, Mr. von Blum."

"*Doctor*, if you must."

"You want me to call you doctor?"

"Preferable to *mister*, but if you don't mind *Fritz*

will do. I did not intend insult. For me, Negro, black, colored, Congolese, darkie, kaffir, African-American— they are all the same. In German, *nigger* is not a bad word, merely a description. Maybe that too has changed. I come from a world where there is only one race, of which I am not part, by official decree. So it is hardly possible I carry in me ill-feeling against another. I meant no harm, I assure you."

"Well, just for the record, we don't call it the National Association for the Advancement of Niggers. I know you're new here."

"I love California."

"The climate?"

"As well there are no brown shirts marching in the streets, and that I can work in film, movies as you say, for a number of years now not a possibility in Germany. *Ubi bene, ibi patria.*"

"Come again?"

"Where it is good, there is one's country. Please tell me about this film. Mr. Shelupsky is paying me, so we should commence our labors. We will enjoy working together, no?"

"I don't know that anyone enjoys working for EZ."

"*Forsan et haec olim meminisse iuvabit.*"

"Over my head."

"An idiom?"

"An idiom. Means: I don't comprehend."

"Not a problem, Larry. Soon you will be speaking Latin like Augustus. *Forsan et haec olim meminisse iuvabit.* Perhaps even this will one day be pleasant to look back upon."

III

What Mr. Shelupsky was paying Fritz was $100 a week, slave wages by Hollywood standards but more than respectable at a time when high-school teachers made that much in a month. Still, Fritz wasn't a high-school teacher but a screenwriter with credits from Berlin to Vienna. Beyond the kind of ethical twinge that never lived long in Hollywood, I felt the strange form of guilt that inspires not one's conscience but one's fear: if EZ could do this to von Blum, he could do it to von Bell-ringer. It was something like the fear that would be attributed to thoughtful but passive Christians in Germany: Today they come for the Saturday people, tomorrow they will come for the Sunday people. Worse, after working with Fritz for only three hours, it was clear he was the pro and I the amateur. I had made eleven films for EZ at Racetrack, but they were hardly art, unless writing snappy dialogue for Buck Brown, our reigning western star, could be considered cowboy verse. Fritz had collaborated on *The Blue Angel*, had been a contract writer for UFA, working with F.W. Murnau, G.W. Pabst and another Fritz—Lang. He was an old drinking buddy of Billy Wilder, who many years later told me at a party that he had learned a basic lesson from Fritz: "An actor enters through a door, you've got nothing—an actor enters through a window, you've got a situation." Fritz and Marlene Dietrich used to do cocaine together. On top of that, the man had written five novels (most Hollywood writers had never read that many), and in his spare time had been a columnist—a cultural columnist, no less, until the Nazis took over—for *Die Welt*, which in its pre-Hitler heyday made our L.A. papers look like the *Ozark Bugle*. So I was less concerned with my partner's skills than with the bigger picture: In the interstice between Fritz's leaving and my walking to Schwab's, just across Crescent Heights Boulevard, for a pack of Luckies, I had a chance to reflect on the risk I was taking. EZ Shelupsky did not tolerate losses.

If my idea failed for a new direction at Racetrack, EZ would boot me so far off the lot I'd never again see so much as a hundred bucks a week. I was an educated Negro with expensive tastes in clothes, whiskey, residence and men. Where was I to go if EZ tossed me out? The white studios were unlikely to hire me. What was I supposed to do, work for a living? The WPA had just dumped three-quarters of a million men off government payrolls. As we used to say in the Party, "On a clear day in Hollywood you can see the class struggle."

These trepidations occupied my mind as I let myself back into the bungalow to find a stranger sitting on my green leather sofa behind what had been a locked door.

"Good afternoon, Mr. Bellringer," the stranger said.

Even seated he was clearly of good size, maybe six-foot-four-inches, with an athletic heft to his shoulders. His tan shoes were shined to perfection, and suitably large, as was the hat on the sofa next to him, a putty-colored fedora with a thin band of light-blue silk that picked up his eyes, which were kind, though whether by nature or intent I could not tell. His jaw was square, his mouth soft, almost permanently puckered, but his nose was aggressive, like a fighter's. His hair was brushed straight back and shiny black. No Easterner, his deep even tan was years in the making. I tried to put all this together, including the charcoal suit, a soft fabric, maybe cashmere, fashionably single-breasted and top-stitched, that must have cost a mint. John Garfield meets Cary Grant meets John Wayne? I couldn't peg him. Could he be a cop? Instantly I catalogued what was in my bungalow and felt the fear of the occasional pot-smoker, then instantly relaxed. In that suit, if this was a cop I was Mae West.

"Do I know you?"

"Allen Sloane." Getting up off the couch, the man was bigger, broader. He seemed to fill the room. His hand reached around mine like a ratchet. "Please excuse my coming in this way. The nice people in the lobby let me in. Told them I was your cousin."

"You're white."

"Some people don't look at these things."

"Really? I never seem to meet them." Then it came to me. It was just a name out of the Los Angeles phone directory, unless you recognized it. I recognized it now, though I would have imagined him different, an Edward G. Robinson, not a George Raft. "Oh, *that* Allen Sloane," I said. "Yes, please sit down. Can I get you something? I don't know what I have. Gin. Bourbon. I may have some rye."

"Don't drink during the day," Sloane said. "I do smoke."

I watched my guest slip a flat gold cigarette case out of his right-hand jacket pocket, flip it open with the same hand and then, with a speed and grace that made it seem easy, light up a Viceroy—it was the only brand with a filter-tip in those days—with a matching gold lighter that magically appeared in his left. I pushed an ashtray full of yesterday's butts toward the man, who smiled regally. "I hear you're doing a script for EZ Shelupsky," Sloane said.

"How do you know that?"

"In my business, you have to know everything."

"Because it's not, you know, *known*."

"I'm sure you'll do well with it. I saw *The Sepia Stranger*. Liked it a lot. Very good dialogue. Jazzy."

Script-writers rarely hear compliments, unless they are nominated for an Oscar, something that I often dreamed of but, considering my situation, might never occur. Well, maybe it would with this one—a film that wasn't made, from a script that wasn't written, off a treatment that was only in my head, and which itself was so far little more than a pleasant blur waiting to be formed by an émigré German Jew who spouted Latin. In pursuing this I had neglected to ask myself the obvious question: What was a white man doing looking at race films? "You don't have to lie on my account."

"I never lie," Sloane said, quite seriously. "I make a habit of it."

"In the film business you might have to, from time to time."

"That's why I'm not in the film business," Sloane said.

"Sometimes I wish I could say that. You get like a hop-head. They give you lots of money, you spend it because that's what you do out here, then you need more and you're pretty much at their mercy." For the life of me, I had no idea why I was saying this. I didn't know Sloane, except by reputation, and would never have said this kind of thing to my own friends. But there was something in Allen Sloane that made me feel he could be relied upon. Maybe the man could have me killed—no maybe: *certainly* Sloane could have me killed—but he wouldn't betray a confidence. That was what they said. I believed it. "What can I do for you, Mr. Sloane?"

"Well, let's say we can do for each other."

"That would be . . .nice."

"Wouldn't it?"

I took a pack of Luckies out of my pocket, fumbled with the match, lit up on the second try. We smoked for a while, the haze rising as our silence filled the void between us, binding us perhaps, until Sloane ground out his butt decisively in the filthy ashtray.

"I'm fucking EZ Shelupsky's lady," he said.

"I beg your pardon, Mr. Sloane?"

"Please. *Allen*."

"Allen. That's not something I need to know."

"It's all right, Larry. We're in love."

"I mean, Mr. Sloane—"

"Allen."

"Allen. I mean, it's not something I'm comfortable with."

"I understand." He reached up slowly with his right hand and scratched his right ear, then his left. They were actually quite small, too small for a man that big. "Why not tell *me* a secret then? Something personal."

"I'd rather not."

"But I told you one."

"Still . . ."

"You could tell me a little secret."

"Allen . . ."

"Or maybe not. You could tell me what I do know. You could tell me you're a Commie."

"That's not true."

"Don't ever lie to me, Larry." Sloane shifted on the sofa so that his head was tilted back, his blue eyes darkening at that angle, as though seeking perspective. "You're not going to lie to me, are you?"

"No."

"You're a card-carrying member of the American Communist Party—is that right or wrong?"

"It's not . . .wrong—exactly."

"Right or wrong, Larry?"

"Mr. Sloane . . ."

"Allen."

"Allen, it's right, but . . ."

"But not something that's going to help you with the EZ Shelupsky's of this town, is that it?"

"In a nutshell."

"And you're a homo."

I felt I was floating down a river, the current taking me where it would. "I'm not sure I know what you mean."

"You're asking for a diagram? You're a colored queer, right or not?"

"I see myself more as a sexually emancipated Negro, but it's not worth the argument."

Sloane laughed. His teeth were large, and the bit of unevenness to them gave him a young look, as though unfinished, but only for a moment. His eyes opened wider, searching out mine. "The last thing I'd want is to argue about it, Larry. Pretty much we define ourselves."

"If this is blackmail, Allen—"

"I don't go in for that, Larry. Aside from some troubles I've had with certain stupid laws that shouldn't be on the books, I'm an honest man. I wouldn't do anything like that. It's just that I told you a secret, and I want you to know I trust you with it. You should trust me with yours. Also I know you're close to broke, or maybe already there, and you need this money off Shelupsky. And a fresh chance. We both need something off EZ Shelupsky."

"I understood she's a lez."

"Who?"

"Nora Bright."

"I heard that, too," Sloane said.

"She's not?"

"I'd rather not talk about Mrs. Shelupsky," Sloane said, as though I had brought her up.

This took a moment to deal with. "Mr. Sloane, Allen . . .I don't know what this has to do with me."

"You don't?" Sloane said. "Well, maybe you don't. But as soon as you stop looking like you swallowed something not kosher, Larry, I'll tell you. In fact, I'll tell you in my car."

"In your car?" I had visions of scenes I myself had written, cheap scenes that ended predictably, and not well. But it didn't make sense. Why would Allen Sloane want to kill me? And if he did, why not right here? And why this business of secrets?

"It's not like you think, Larry," Sloane said with a big grin as he stood, towering over me and dominating the sunny, unkempt room like one of those palms in West-lake Park where Wilshire Boulevard slices right through it. They renamed it MacArthur Park after the war, but the palms are still there. "You like the ponies, right?"

"The ponies?"

"Horses."

"I sometimes, I mean, I used to..."

"Come on, Larry. Get your hat. I'm going to intro-duce you to a horse."

IV

There was no question which was Allen Sloane's car outside on Havenhurst Drive. There were probably no more than a dozen LaSalle convertible coupes in California. Two years before, in 1937, the same car, a V-8, had set a speed and endurance record at the Indianapolis Speedway of 82 miles per hour. This one was the same baby-blue as Sloane's tie and hat band, the seats a fawn mohair, the eggshell linen top bright as a boiled shirt. "Long drive?" I asked. We passed my own parked black '34 Ford with a *whoosh*, the LaSalle's engine purring, barely at work. "Where we're headed?"

"Two months ago I was returning back from Rosarita Beach," Sloane said, as if in answer. "With friends. You know Rosarita?"

"Below Tijuana."

"Been there?"

"Not really," I said.

Sloane took his eyes off the road for a moment and gave me a look. "Larry . . ."

"I mean, no. I've been to Tee. Never got to Rosarita."

"I'll fly you down sometime. Rosarita Beach Hotel, they have an airstrip. Otherwise, it's very rustic and romantic. Like L.A. was maybe in the last century. Usually I take my plane, but the weather was bad. When I go down to Agua Caliente—that you know?"

"I've invested a bit of money there."

"You know what they say about Tijuana—the liquor's cheap, the women cheaper, but the ponies . . .expensive."

I was being patronized. I didn't mind. It was better than threatened. It was better than ignored. Just as riding along toward the San Fernando Valley in a luxe coupe was better than walking. These last weeks before I had climbed back on EZ's payroll, when I could walk that's what I did: gas was up to ten cents a gallon, and the Ford, whether from engine-wear or a slow leak, drank it. I looked out through the spotless windshield of the LaSalle at orderly rows of orange trees, a noble but ragged stand of walnuts, then more citrus with big leaves, grapefruit maybe. Go ahead, patronize me, Mr. Sloane. But at least I'm not screwing another man's wife. Of course, I had more than once screwed someone's husband. "You were saying, about Rosarita?"

"Exactly," Sloane said, the big car sailing silently along under his hand like a toy boat windborne on a lake in some quiet park. "We were down at the track, laid over at Rosarita, went fishing—you like deep-sea, Larry?"

"Never been."

"You'd love it. Very satisfying, except to the fish. On the way back, a funny thing happens."

"Funny?"

"Driving by the border, where they wave you through—you know where, the booths and all—Border Patrol stops the car."

"This car?"

"A different one. We were six in the party. This one's tight on space in the back. You can see that."

"What happened?"

"I got arrested."

"For what?"

"Entering the country illegally." He paused. "You may not believe this, Larry. I hardly believe it myself, but it turns out I talk like an American, pay taxes like an American, dress like an American, look like an American, fuck like an American. But I'm not an American."

"You're not?"

"I'm a Russian, or maybe a Canadian. Do I look Russian or Canadian to you?"

"You look American."

"Damn right, but the authorities—you know what that means, government by the rich people, of the rich people, for the rich people– they do what they want."

Even I, who had bought wholesale into what by then I was beginning to suspect were the lies of the American Communist Party—Hitler and Stalin had signed a pact just days earlier; so much for the evils of fascism—would have to be a lot more stupid than to buy into the legitimacy of this view from a man wearing a hand-tailored cashmere suit, a $100 hat and driving one of the most expensive cars you could buy without having it custom-made by European elves. Any wise-guy could carry a gold cigarette case and lighter, but the car was no window-dressing. Nor was the set-up we now turned into.

It was a horse farm, a big one. On either side of the unmarked gravel road that wound from the highway were dozens of them, beautiful horses, some approaching the white three-board fence to get close to the car and others high-tailing across the green paddocks like so many studies in independence. Horses are like people: some are drawn to power, others run from it. At the moment I did not know which of these I was.

"What do you mean, a Russian?"

"Or a Canadian. Turns out I wasn't born in this country. My parents—I didn't know them a long time, a kid when they died, so I never got the real story—they left Russia, Minsk, White Russia, wherever the hell that is, and came to Toronto before they arrived in the US. Either I was born in one place or the other, Russia or Canada. Or maybe on the boat. The S.S. Savoie was the boat, that much I know, so maybe I'm a frog. All along, I thought I was American. Like I say, turns out I'm not. That means the FBI—and don't kid yourself, but it's the FBI; that faggot Hoover, no offense intended, has it in for me—wants to ship me to the Soviet Union. Would you want to go live in Russia, Larry?"

"They're doing some really good things."

"Yeah, sure. But I don't see you picking up and moving to Moscow. Do me a favor, do yourself a favor. Don't bullshit me. If you and your Commie friends really wanted to go live in the workers' paradise you wouldn't be here. You'd be there."

"I'm an American."

"Lucky you. You know, in Russia there's no gambling. It's not only illegal—hell, it's illegal here—but there's only one track you can bet at in the whole country, and no gambling action away from that track, which is understandable because placing a $2 bet anywhere else can get you twenty years in Siberia. Anyway, nobody has an extra *ruble* in their pocket. Larry, they don't even have pockets. I heard that: they make coats without pockets to save money because nobody has what to put in them anyway. There's no toilet paper in the whole country, just newspaper, and you have to be careful you don't wipe your ass with Stalin's picture because that's a crime. Also it happens I don't speak the language. I got a hope for Cuba, but the feds are already leaning on the top people there. You know how they got the Cubans to turn away that boat with the nine hundred Jews and they're sailing around and nobody will take them, because nobody wants what they call *refujews* . . ."

"The St. Louis."

"Because Washington doesn't want them hanging around in Cuba waiting for a U.S. visa? Well, if J. Edgar Hoover doesn't want Allen Sloan in Cuba, you think those greaseballs are going to say no? So what does that leave me, Panama? Nothing personal, but that's practically an African country. The Canadians won't take me. I'd accept going to Canada—how bad can that be?—but it seems as though the Royal Canadian Mounted Police, that's like the FBI on horseback, got ahold of my jacket."

For a moment I heard *coat*, not *record*. "Gambling?"

"Gambling, this and that. Nothing serious. You know, when I was younger I was more rough around the edges than I am now. I didn't go to Harvard, that's for sure."

I took it as it came. I could stand on my head and explain how I'd been admitted to Harvard on my grades and because, long ago in another life, I'd been pretty good with an *épée* as a high-school fencer in Dobbs Ferry, NY. Despite my skin color, to the Sloanes and Shelupskys of this world I came from another one, and had to be punished for it. For crying out loud, my dad was a school teacher, and his was a dirt-farmer. And I can't get a hotel room in most cities in this country. But saying that would be useless. They were dealing with a Harvard man, a whole other class. As if, despite what the Party preached, class meant a damn thing. It never failed to amaze me the kind of class money could buy. This house, for instance.

A crescent driveway led right to the front porch, from which hung a plank sign in faux western script: Dark Horse Ranch. California houses were big; this was sprawling. Long and low to the ground, it seemed to reach out to both ends of the horizon.

"You want to see the pony?" Sloane asked. "Or a cold drink first?"

A gin-and-tonic delivered by a Mexican servant in a white jacket over dungarees and cowboy boots hit the spot, but the horse was even better. Small for a thoroughbred at maybe fifteen and a half hands, this was a gray stallion with four white socks, a fine long head and ears that seemed to be in conversation with each other.

There is something about a great horse. You can't explain it or describe it, but when you see it you know right away. Alone in the paddock, it grazed peacefully, ignoring the visitors but clearly cognizant, not wary exactly, yet conscious enough of their presence to keep one eye cocked. A stallion, all right. There was no mistaking that, his business emerging pink and semi-erect like a salami in the window of Cantor's Delicatessen, the one in Boyle Heights, before they moved to Fairfax. His silken skin was stretched tight and nearly translucent over pneumatic muscles that appeared to be constrained only by momentary indolence, a living version of the automobile in the driveway, whose energy was evident even when it stood still. "Nice animal," I said. "You race him?"

"Wish I could, Larry. He's a champion, but the same people who say I'm not an American say he can't run on a thoroughbred track in the U.S. of A. In fact, he can't run on a quarter-horse track like they have out in New Mexico and Texas either. He was just born on the wrong side of the tracks, you might say."

I doubted I might say that, ever. Sometimes it seemed I was the only person I knew in L.A. who spoke the kind of English that was not learned from the movies. "No papers?"

"Not a one," Sloane said. "But he's fast enough to beat anything on four feet they have out here on the coast, and probably eastern horses too. Some people have got ahold of the sport, and they won't let it go. The horses have to be in the studbook, thoroughbreds, as if there's anything like that in the real world. In the real world, Larry, even guys like me have a chance. Maybe I had a few bad breaks, my life didn't start out easy, and this thing with the immigration it's no laughable matter either. But let's say a smart guy can land on his feet or, if he's lucky, on someone else's."

Was it a joke? "He's that fast?"

"You know what I think?" Sloane asked, not waiting for an answer. "I think that if out here they ever get lip-tattooing—they're starting it in the east, you can't race at

Belmont without your horse having it—then it's going to be impossible to switch a horse in a race. I mean, look at this horse and look at a nag that looks just like him, except with zero ambition, owned by someone like EZ Shelupsky. OK, this one's ears curve a little more toward each other, and maybe the white socks climb up a little higher over the fetlocks, but basically these are two gray stallions on the small side, and the only difference anyone could see is ours has the bigger dick. Maybe you being a queer could spot that, nothing personal, but in general the only time this would come into question, it would be a mare who would notice, and she'd have to be servicing both stallions, and she'd have to talk English in the bargain. So I don't think that's going to happen."

"You're going to switch this horse?"

"If I can."

Something was coming into focus, as it does in a screenplay when you realize what the plot hinges on. "With one of Shelupsky's?"

"Why not?"

"He wouldn't let it happen. He'd be washed up if it did, and he doesn't need the money."

"Maybe he doesn't, Larry, but I do. Besides, who's asking EZ fucking Shelupsky?"

If ideas for a movie came to me as quickly, I'd probably have been a lot richer. This one simply appeared in my brain, sudden as an uninvited guest. "Me?'

"Nah," Sloane said. "But you might come out ahead if you play your cards right."

I did not want to ask what would happen if I didn't. At cards Allen Sloane was the professional, not me. "How did you know what I'm working on?"

"The Jew movie?"

"Yes," I said. "The Jew movie."

"I told you, EZ's lady told me."

"But she's a lez."

"No, she isn't."

"She's famously a lez, Mr. Sloane. Allen. We see each other at the same clubs."

"I'm not talking about EZ Shelupsky's wife, Larry. I'm talking about his lady."

"You lost me."

"You went to Harvard? They didn't teach you the difference?" He smiled. "You want to know who she is, don't you?"

"Part of me does."

"The other part is the one to listen to. That would be the smart part. Let's just say if anyone knew about it there'd be trouble for Shelupsky, and maybe trouble for me."

For a moment, it was difficult to speak. I knew what Sloane was hinting at. Whoever the "lady" was she had lured Shelupsky across the color line, or he her. Just a whiff of it would make EZ *producer non grata* at every party in Los Angeles. Maybe it was 1939, maybe a year earlier Joe Louis had kayoed Max Schmeling, maybe if Roosevelt got us into a war black soldiers would be as good as white, but in the film industry 1939 might as well have been 1839. "You're telling me EZ Shelupsky is fucking a—"

"I am."

"How do you know that, if you don't mind my asking?"

"I don't mind," Sloane said, looking at once proud and vulnerable, as though he, not I, had stepped out of the closet. "Because I'm fucking her, too. I told you that."

"You did."

"Except I'm fucking her better."

V

On the third day Fritz showed up at my bungalow with a request. Naturally, it was cloaked in Latin. *"Duo cum faciunt idem, non est idem."*

"When two make . . .?"

"When two *do* the same. . ."

"When two do the same, it isn't the same."

"Precisely. My dear Larry, your Latin improves."

"You're saying?"

"Larry, my dear, please. Let me create structure. You will make dialogue to hang upon it, like lights on a tree."

"I thought that was the plan."

Fritz lit a Chesterfield and began strolling around my living room like a retiree whiling away his afternoon in a park. Round and round he went, the ash growing on his cigarette until it fell. I didn't mind. I must have missed that class in queer school. Anyway, the floors were terra cotta. Twice a week a maid came in and cleaned up the mess. "But we have been ignoring this distinction. I need from you only a clear tale, a story. Beginning, middle, end. Think of it not as a film. It is a story."

"But it is a film, Fritz." I corrected myself. "Movie."

"It will be, but first it must be a story. Tell it."

"I thought I did."

The little man ground his butt out in the ashtray and immediately lit another, holding it in that peculiar European way, between thumb and forefinger, like a freshly plucked tic. *"Ab Jove principium."*

"Jove is Jupiter. That much I got."

Fritz shook his head. "I don't know what you were doing all the years—four? five? *six?*—in Harvard. Latin should be taught from grade one. In kindergarten, no? Yes, of course: Jupiter. *Ab Jove principium.* Start with Jupiter. That is, with the most important."

"I thought I did."

"Bis repetita non placent. Repetition is not well received. I shall ask again, Larry. What is the point of this film?"

Did movies have points? This was new to me, and troubling. I had spent four years creating scripts whose only intent was to entertain, and thus make money. Now this refugee in a ridiculously out-of-date suit, not even a citizen, was telling me there had to be a point. "It's a movie, Fritz. You know why Hollywood hasn't made a movie about someone dying of cancer? They can't figure out where to stick in the conga line."

"Credo cria absurdum. I believe it because it is absurd. But our mission is to tell a story. If the story is good it will entertain. *Praevenire melius est quam praeveneri."*

"It is better to precede," I said, working it out—some phrases were easier than others. "Than to be preceded."

"Excellent! My dear Larry, let us not worry about what Hollywood has done. You know what we say in Germany? All but the first dog have the same view. If we do our jobs correctly, Hollywood will follow."

"You have an elevated vision of the movie business, Fritz. It's all about the money."

"Of course it is. But we are all about the art. The meeting of the one with the other, that is film. Remember: *Pecunia non olet.* Money—"

"Doesn't smell."

"So give us first the art, then someone else will turn it into money."

Actually, I did not know where to start. Fritz and I had danced around this for the first two days, escaping it actually. I spent a good while asking him about being a Jew in Germany, he asking me about being a colored man in America. We agreed on this much: it was better to be a live nigger in Mississippi than a dead kike in Bavaria. Unfortunately, talking endlessly of our personal troubles did not get us far in working through a difficult professional situation. I set out to try again. "Bare bones, right?"

"Bare, bare. Bleached."

"We have the main story. It's about the first shipload of Jews to come to North America, which it turns out is not true, because we have the second story, which actually should be the first. Because Jews were coming here with the Spanish, only they weren't Jews. They were secret Jews—"

"*Marannos*. A charming word, it means pigs."

"Does it?"

"You don't know Spanish either?"

"I took two years of high-school Latin. At college–"

"The Heidelberg of Massachusetts."

"At Harvard, two years of French. Can we skip the educational rank-pulling and get on with this?"

"Rank-pulling?"

"Tell you later. So what we have is a Spanish priest who is a secret Jew, because all the Jews who remained in Spain had to become Christians, and he's about to be arrested by the Inquisition, so he hops a galleon for the new world, New Spain, which is Mexico, where he settles in with the horses that he has brought over—"

"Raising horses was the family business in Spain, very good."

"Which are very special horses—the mustangs are descended from them—which are called the Izquierda Line."

"Which we can not call them, my dear Larry, because in these times . . ."

"It *is* the name of the line of horses. This is based on a true story. The Izquierda Line."

"But it means the line of the left."

"Does it?"

"You live in a city that is half Mexican and you do not know this? Right, left. In any language it is the first thing one learns."

"I talk to the maid in English."

"Very nice," Fritz said. "In Los Angeles the nigger of the nigger is the Mexican."

"Moving right along," I said. "We're looking at this priest in Mexico City in, say, 1590, and he comes to realize the Inquisition is here too. Somehow we have to explain the Inquisition, burning Jews . . . There's just too much back story here."

"Tell the *entire* story, dear Larry. We shall work later on which part is front, which is back, which is gold, which shit. How does our priest discover he is once more in danger?"

"Maybe the same official of the Inquisition that was on to him in Spain arrives in Mexico."

"Excellent. A good visual. We now have three seconds of film."

"So he realizes he has to get out of Dodge."

"An automobile?"

"Get out of Mexico City. So he attaches himself and his horses—"

"How many horses?"

"I really don't know, Fritz. Got to be at least two, male and female, otherwise the rest of the story doesn't make sense."

"An uncertain number of horses. Noted."

"So he attaches himself to an expedition heading north to what is now New Mexico, Arizona—we could show a map."

"We could. Or not. The main thing: *Periculum in mora.*"

I looked at him. He was lighting one Chesterfield from the butt of another. And I thought I was a heavy smoker. We all were then. "Which means?"

"There is danger in delay. For our purposes excellent. Nothing drives a film, excuse me, movie, better than fear. He is traveling with Christians. *Una solis victis, nullam sperare salutem.* Do not bother to translate this one: The only safety for the defeated is to relinquish all hope of safety. The man is desperate. Where can he go? Nowhere but where there is even more danger. Does our priest have a name?"

"Father Antonio. When he comes to New York, Nieuw Amsterdam, in the next part with the Jews from Brazil, he is called Abraham. He goes back to being a Jew. We have to show how he gets from Mexico to Brazil, where he doesn't have to live as a Christian, but it's Father Antonio in this part."

"We can do better."

"But that is his real name, Fritz. It really is based on a—"

"And if his real name were Franklin Delano Roosevelt, would we use it?"

"But it wasn't."

Fritz ground out his Chesterfield, barely smoked, in the large ashtray on the coffee table, opened his collar and released the knot in his necktie, so that it hung around his neck like a shawl. *"Aquila non capit muscas."*

"The eagle . . .something . . .muscles."

"The eagle does not hunt flies, my dear boy. *Muscas, not musclas.* Let us not worry the details. Tell the story."

"Fritz, if you'd *let* me tell the story. . ."

"Tell it, tell it." The little man sat down heavily on my green leather couch, put his feet up on the coffee table, and squeezed his eyes shut. "For you to tell, for me to imagine."

Now it was my turn to pace. I took a walk to the window, where I had a view of part of the pool. A young man in his 20s, a claim that I would be able to make only several months more, was climbing to the diving platform. I watched him flex the board, arc, then sail out of sight. My view was blocked by another bungalow. It was as if he had disappeared. It was 4 p.m. I would have liked to join the young man at the pool. You never knew. But even in the Garden of Allah, where the management rented to coloreds, to one colored in fact because there was no other such tenant—few Negroes could afford what I was paying: you could get a whole house in South Central for a quarter of what it cost to rent this bungalow—showing up at the pool in a swimsuit would be pushing it. There was one standard for a Negro in a suit and tie, another for one mostly naked. I could have used a swim, a cocktail, mindless banter, flirtation, the touch of flesh. A soft purring noise from behind turned me around. "Fritz?" I said softly. But he made no move. He was asleep.

VI

A day later at Hollywood Park, EZ Shelupsky invited me to dine with him on filet mignon so rare the chef laughed to his friends that it had merely glanced at the frying pan—one thing about being colored in L.A.: you always have access to the kitchen. The chef knew how Shelupsky liked his meat—"black and blue"—because EZ had sent back two steaks when the track opened in June the year before. There was no protesting. A director of the Hollywood Park Racing Association, EZ Shelupsky paid his salary. EZ knew how he liked his meat and therefore, by unsolicited extension, how I would have mine, blood and all.

Dictating precisely how our meat reached the table may have been one of the few things he could control that season at Hollywood Park. EZ's movies made lots of money, he was driven around L.A. in a super-long, hand-made maroon-and-black Brewster with a raked heart-shaped grill, and his wife, whatever she did on the side, was regularly cited by *Photoplay* as one of America's ten most-beautiful women. But for months EZ had not saddled a winner. Now, sitting with his trainer, Ozzie Hirsch, who had trained the best horseflesh in the West, with winners in the Preakness and the Belmont Stakes and four times horses in the money in the Kentucky Derby, Shelupsky devoured his steak with a feverish intensity and with his eyes seemed about to devour Hirsch. This was as pleasant to watch as a tiger toying with a lamb, but compelling.

"Mr. Shelupsky," the trainer said now, fiddling nervously with his trout. He was being treated like a nigger, and he didn't like it, especially with a real specimen of that race sitting as an equal opposite. "Things goes in waves."

"Tell me more stories, Oz. How much money I pay you?"

"It's not the money." Hirsch said. "It's just the way it is. If you paid me double and you spent ten times as much for stock we could still be this way. You only got to wait it out."

Shelupsky polished off his steak, smeared the white napkin, still folded on the table, across his mouth, leaving it stained pink from blood, picked up the gold-plated Zeiss field glasses Nora had given him for his birthday, and watched a chestnut mare cross the finish line, then another horse, then two more, neck and neck, then a fourth, then a fifth, then . . . his, a smallish gray with four white socks and, were he human, what could only be called an expression of bottomless apathy. "The steak I just ate could beat this nag you got me, Ozzie. If you was a writer you wouldn't be on the lot. But I have faith in you."

"Thank you, Mr. Shelupsky."

"Only not forever."

When Oz Hirsch left the table, his fish lying there on the black-and-red Hollywood Park plate, explored but not eaten, EZ turned his attention to me: same tiger, fresh lamb. "You know what I pay him?"

"No, EZ, I don't."

"Good you don't. But you know what I pay you. I got something to see for that?"

"Fritz and I are working on it."

"Is there a writer in this city ever got paid for six weeks that he didn't turn in a script on the last day?"

I allowed myself the luxury of a shrug. If this were all that was bothering EZ Shelupsky, I could stand it. "EZ, this isn't exactly *Colored Cowpokes of Colorado*."

"I hope not. Larry, how can I say this delicately?"

"Are you going to try?"

"No," EZ said. "Why the fuck should I? I'm paying you, not the other way around. It's like this: the Negro audience, I love them with all my heart and also my wallet, but they're a simple audience. They want a laugh, they want a song, a little tap-dancing, a hero, a girl-hero, and happily ever after. The Jewish audience, they have a certain attitude. When the people of the book go to the movies, you can't buy them off with chorus girls and Cab Calloway. Explain me one thing I don't understand."

I sliced what was left of my filet into slivers, each one oozing red. EZ's own plate was wiped clean. He had used a roll to mop up the pool of blood. Maybe he really was a tiger. "If I can."

"Why is it I'm making a movie about the American Jews, and for the American Jews, and who do I have writing it but a colored and a kraut? Am I crazy or what? Give me one reason I shouldn't pay you off right now, you and Fritz von whatever together, and give the whole thing over to a real Jew, or two or three. For what I'm paying you, I could get a *minion*."

"You know why, EZ," I said with more confidence than I felt. "First off, you trust me, both to do top-class work, on time and ready to shoot, and because you know I won't talk to *The Hollywood Reporter* or *Variety* and give your competitors a chance to catch up."

"Maybe you *should* be a producer, Larry. But tell me the truth, man to man. Do you really know enough about being a Jew? Last time I looked, you're a colored—granted a Harvard colored. And that Fritz, I never saw a Jew like that in my life. Every other word comes out of his mouth, it's ancient Greek. How can two guys like you carry this thing off? Be honest with me, Larry. We're almost like friends. Pretend you're not in the movie business—tell the truth."

"You know, EZ, that the NAACP was founded by Jews?"

"And still bankrolled."

"And Jews are in the forefront in the colored man's struggle for equal rights?"

"So?"

"And there isn't a Negro church in America that doesn't sing hymns right out of Jewish history, right out of the Old Testament. *Let My People Go. Joshua Fit the Battle of Jericho. We Is Comin', Father Abraham.* And look at you, a Jew, and you're running one of the biggest colored businesses in the world. Jews and Negroes, we have quite a bit in common. Hell, EZ, I wouldn't be surprised if your next wife will be just a little on the dark side."

Perhaps I'd gone too far. EZ Shelupsky's face went ashen, and he averted his eyes as though I knew something I shouldn't—which I did, but which he could not possibly know, because if he did he would have to know how I had come by the information, and that would not be pleasant. After a while the studio head seemed to regain his composure. He feigned a smile, looked directly at me, and said, "Equal but separate, that's the way it should be, Larry. I don't think intermarriage is a good thing. People should stay with their own."

"You married a gentile."

"A white gentile, Larry, and a wonderful, loving woman."

I'd heard from my dyke friends just how wonderful. "I'm sure she is."

"And unlike many people in California, I'm not looking to keep changing partners. I'll leave that to the wildcats and the homos who can't settle down."

"I know homos who have."

"Can't last, Larry. You know that. The homo is driven by sex. One partner can't cut the ketchup. And the wildcats, I think they just learned from the homos. I don't mean to offend. But it's the truth."

There was little to say to that. EZ Shelupsky, up to this moment an imperial monster—all powerful, all knowing, all consuming—had revealed a part of himself whose sadness and fear would probably haunt him to his grave. I had long before come to terms with what I was, but EZ Shelupsky would deny in his soul what his heart required and thus compromised would struggle within himself, taking the pleasure he demanded and feeling shame, then not taking that pleasure and feeling within himself the cold emptiness of a life unlived, a solitude unrelieved.

For a long while we sat in silence in the red-and-black wicker easychairs in the clubhouse shade while a new set of horses was guided into the starting gate, a shot was fired, and the track announcer described the fluid chaos that before our eyes formed itself into an elongated arrowhead, at whose tip a horse and rider came flying across our field of view, followed by a second, a third, then a pack, then stragglers, then nothing but dust.

"That fourth horse," EZ said, putting down his field glasses. "That's mine. Every nag I got these days finishes out of the money. You know what? I don't feel sad for myself, certainly not for that Hirsch who gets paid plenty to give me losers, but for the poor horses. A horse runs to win, just like us, Larry. And if we don't win, God help us, we're losers."

Once again, I knew more than I could let on. "Not to worry, EZ. You'll have a winner soon."

VII

Fritz von Blum dozed off at the same hour every afternoon, so most of our work had to be done by four. Neither alcohol nor coffee nor cigarettes could keep him from his regular nap. After a week I became accustomed to use his nap-time to take a walk down the irregularly paved, palm-lined flagstone path out past the pool where the pretty youth had staked out a corner with his pretty friends—they were apparently a crew of new contract players with MGM, which every year brought over enough young British actors on the bet maybe one or two would make it, the others to be unceremoniously dropped; they were put up in the main house, whose rooms were dark, and thus known as the Hallroom Boys. After making eye contact or not, I'd walk out through the main entrance down to Schwab's for a couple of packs of smokes, Luckies for me, Chesterfield for Fritz, glance at the front page of the *Examiner*—*Packard to Debut Air-Conditioned Car*; *Cincinnati Wins National League Race—To Face Yankees Minus Gehrig in Series*; *"Wizard of Oz" Opens Big at Grauman's Chinese*; *King George Tells Press He "Rather Likes Hot-Dogs" After U.S. Visit*; *Germany Closes All Jewish Firms*—and then make my way back to the Garden of Allah, past the pretty Hallroom Boys by the pool, to waken Fritz. He never stirred when I came in, but by the time the coffee was cooked you could see him coming to. I wasn't sure whether it was the percolator pop-pop-popping or the sweet, steamy smell of the coffee. He drank it black, with enough sugar to sink a battleship in Pearl Harbor. In two years, that would actually happen.

But it was still only three, an hour to go before Fritzi conked out, and I was already looking forward to my stroll to Schwab's. We were getting nowhere, slowly.

"*Dura necessitatus,*" he said.

"Necessity is hard," I said. Little by little, my Latin was coming back. "*Dura Hollywoodus.*"

"Not so harsh, Hollywood," he said, stifling a yawn. "Compared to what I left."

"That's our story," I offered back. "Man leaves what he knows for what he doesn't, because what he knows is going to kill him."

"You think Hitler will kill the Jews?"

"Never happen," I said. "What's he going to do, burn them? He's more or less stuck with the Jews unless the U.S. lets them in, which we won't. Anyway, if he did get rid of all the Jews, he'd have a hard time selling his program. It's like what would happen to the Klan if suddenly there weren't any Negroes. Frankly, Fritz, I have trouble understanding how come the Jews are hated so much. What makes them hated like that?" I wanted to say *you* for *them*, but it would sound too much like what I was thinking: How come the Germans hate you so much, Fritz, when all you are is a pudgy Latin-spouting screenwriter who is about as much threat to anyone as one of EZ's inoffensive ponies? "You got family back there?"

"Some." He thought a moment, as though reviewing faces in an album.

"They don't want to leave?"

"Someone has to take them," he said. "You know the most expensive word in German? *Visa.*"

"What about Palestine?"

"Sewed up tight. You can try to run the British blockade, but if you are apprehended it is not a pleasure to be sent back."

"You made it out."

He shrugged. "America needs screenwriters with good Latin," he said. "Let us go on with our story."

"Where are we?"

"Father Antonio has joined an expedition to the north, ostensibly to promote Christianity, but in reality to escape the Inquisition, which has followed him to Mexico—"

"In the person of the same priest who was on to him already in Seville."

"Larry, my dear, I know just how to play this. One lingering shot as Father Antonio, he is still Father Antonio, sees said nemesis disembarking from a sedan chair—"

"A what?"

"One assumes they had sedan chairs. Or maybe coaches. I prefer the visual decadence of the sedan chair. People carrying people. And we hold that shot, all Father Antonio's eyes, terror, fear, turning wheels, how to escape, what to do. And all this before we know who it is that causes this fear, and then only in the very briefest of shots. So we have seven counts of terrified eyes, and finally only one count of whom he is so terrified to have seen. Merely a blur. This is cinema, Larry. In good cinema, as in bad life, we never know what will happen next."

"I thought I was telling the story."

"My deep apology," Fritz said. "Please."

"So in the next scene we see him hooking up with an expedition to the north to discover treasure, ostensibly to convert the Apache and Navajo tribes of what is now New Mexico and Arizona, but it's really about gold and silver. The expedition runs into trouble from the beginning. We're looking at a hundred men, most of them small-time Spanish aristocrats, the second sons, the ones who didn't inherit title or wealth, who usually became priests, but in those days with the promise of treasure in the new world they become gentleman brigands in a country where there are already dozens of silver and gold mines and maybe hundreds more waiting to be discovered, and plenty of labor to work them. The church won't permit enslaving Christians, so we have this dichotomy, the conquistadors need to keep the Indians unbaptized while the *padres* are there only to baptize them." I paused. "Maybe Father Antonio stands up for the Indians, which puts him at odds with the Spaniards." None of this sounded like a movie. I fell back on what I knew. "Fritz, we need a villain."

He lit a second Chesterfield from the butt in his hand, his fingertips so stained with nicotine they were darker than my own. "Hollywood needs villains, but in the world outside the cinema it is not so simple. Myself, I can understand the second sons. Adventure, romance, riches. Of course they were fools, but some made out well. The first sons, they stayed put, sleeping in their beds. The second sons were sinners, but that is different from villains. *Qui dormit non peccat.* He who sleeps—"

"Doesn't sin."

"Exactly, my dear Larry. So we should avoid feathering and tarring—"

"Tarring and feathering."

"Yes, those who do. Desperation, foolishness, greed. But greed is not evil in itself. We all do damage."

"You're saying a story without a villain? The whole idea is Father Antonio breaks away from the conquistadors, or maybe defends them, or maybe he's challenged by the Spaniards as an Indian-lover, or maybe—"

"We should leave room for . . . uncertainty, no? Clarity in logic, yes, but in art—"

"You know what, Fritz? You ought to know this. Wasn't it Goering who said every time he hears the word *culture* he reaches for his gun . . . "

141

"Hanns Johst. Many people think Hermann Goering, but Goering was quoting Johst. *Wenn ich 'Kultur' höre . . . entsichere ich meinen Browning.* It was in Johst's play 'Schlageter.' Terrible work. Not Goering, but a playwright." He smiled. "Like us."

"Well, every time you say *art* I break out in hives."

His eyes narrowed. "Bees?"

"Skin eruptions. The sweats. Heebie-jeebies. Anxiety."

"Angst."

"Yeah, ohngst. It's very simple. If Father Antonio—later Abraham, when he throws off the cassock—if this guy is going to be a hero, the audience needs to play him off a villain."

"Maybe the times are the villain. You have no sympathy for the second sons?"

"I have no sympathy for lynch mobs, the Klan, human monsters. You have sympathy for Nazis?"

"Not sympathy. But I can understand. Hate is like love. It does not occur in a vacuum. *Auri sacra fames.* The accursed hunger for gold. But they are accursed first."

"If that's the case, there's no good or bad, no heroes and villains, no right and wrong."

Fritz sighed, expelling so much smoke it appeared he might be on fire, that somewhere in his mild depths was a kind of purifying blaze. "You are a Communist, Larry?"

"More or less."

"So you have read *Das Kapital?*"

"Parts."

"I have read it all, which is why I am not a Communist. Have you then looked into Hitler's *Mein Kampf?* Of course not, why should you? But I will tell you something. Stalin, armed with *Das Kapital,* has now signed a pact with Hitler, armed with *Mein Kampf.*

You know what the Romans would have said? *Cave ab homine unius libre.*"

"Beware the man ... of one ... freedom?"

"Beware the man of one book."

"I don't get it."

"These people, these conquistadors, they are poor men, fools. And they do terrible damage. But they were themselves damaged. Would not our story of Father Antonio be stronger, really stronger, if we could show him not as a victim of these fools—fools with swords and guns, primitive guns but guns still, yes, and fools still—but as a hero *within* himself? He leaves the expedition not because they are evil, but because he must find for himself the good."

"And we show that how, visually?"

Fritz rested his too-large head onto the back of my green leather couch. He seemed to be examining the stucco on the ceiling, seeking patterns perhaps. "You are a Communist because of what happened to your people. The Communists promise you this and that, paradise on earth, a world without racism, without perhaps race. And you say, 'I will embrace that.' But in so doing, you embrace another evil."

"I'm sure there is a reason Comrade Stalin signed the pact."

"Certainly. To buy time, perhaps. Build up his military, to take half of Poland, to take other lands, to better negotiate with London and Paris and Washington. Who knows? But in the end, it is evil in a pact with evil. So you are saying, 'Fritzi, better the evil of a Stalin than the evil of Ku Klux Klan.' But I say, 'Larry, doing what is right is better than doing what seems right.' Father Antonio must seek *himself* in the wilderness. He goes to the Apaches with his horses, these special horses, and lives

with them, savages perhaps, but civilized enough not, unlike the Spaniards, to force their own beliefs on a stranger,
and returns to the Judaism of his fathers, throwing off enforced Christianity, giving hope—horses being the physical form of hope—to these poor people so that they may
fight off the—"

"Fritz, it's a fucking movie."

"Ars est celare artem."

"Art is to . . . do something or other . . . to art."

"To conceal! Art is to conceal art!"

"Fritz," I said, picking up my suit jacket and heading
for the door. "I'm going out for some smokes. I know when
I come back you're going to be snoozing. Then I'm going
to make us some coffee. Then we're going to write a fucking *movie* that people—in this case, Jews—are going to
be able to identify with, that they're going to cheer when
they leave the movie house, that they'll tell their friends
about when they go to what-do-you-call-it, temple. It'll
be the pageant of the Jewish people. One: Here is Father
Antonio, and through him we tell the story of the Jews
in Spain, anti-semitism, and he comes to the New World,
supplies the Indians with horses, special horses, and teaches
them riding, training, breeding and what veterinary skills
there were. Two: Fifty years later, a ship turns up in New
York harbor, excuse me, Nieuw Amsterdam (which at least
to you I don't have to fucking explain), and it's come from
Brazil, which the Jews are fleeing, and no one will take
them—echoes of today maybe, but that's what we want, a
strong story with a smell of the headlines—and on that ship
is this young Jewish lawyer who stands up to Peter Stuyvesant
and says the Jews are not leaving until an order comes from
the Dutch East India Company, which has sponsored Nieuw
Amsterdam, and when months later the reply comes back, it

says, 'Let these Hebrews stay,' which of course is because the directors of the Dutch East India Company are Jews, and that's how the Jews came to America. Three: Which we haven't even thought about how to do, is one of the passengers on the ship, the St. Cathriene, is none other than the former Father Antonio, who eventually went down to Brazil to live as a Jew and now for the second time becomes a refugee, and he's telling his story to the Jewish lawyer, who is his son, and to his grandson. So the final part of the story is the grandson grows up in Virginia, and he's a revolutionary, and a horse breeder, and he supplies the fast horses for George Washington's troops. That's it, that's our story, which we have to tell in a hundred minutes."

"Larry, you can't even summarize this tale, these tales, in one hundred minutes, much less visually. Do you know what your Alfred Hitchcock said? The length of a film is determined by the capacity of the human bladder. This is three separate films."

"Movies."

"Movies. To do justice to this, we need a wide, wide, wide canvas, or a triptych, three screens framed together. History is not a travelogue. It is made of human interaction. Go back to Mr. EZ Shelupsky and tell him we have three films."

"I need one treatment for one film, Fritz. And if you can't do it, then I'll go back to EZ and get someone else."

Maybe I expected Latin. What I got was the briefest of all gestures, the little man's little hands, so delicate—it was hard to think they could ever have wielded anything more than a pen (that was a dueling scar on his cheek; Fritz had been a member of the Jewish dueling society at

Heidelberg)—both hands turning out, palms raised. Was it resignation, refusal, helplessness? I couldn't make it out, and I had stopped caring. I went out down the flagstone path past the pool. The beautiful young Hallroom Boys were gone. It was coolish, overcast, about to rain. On the way back the skies opened up. I used that day's *Examiner* as an umbrella. It soaked up the downpour so that when I got back only the large black headlines were legible: Hitler had invaded Poland.

VIII

Three weeks later when a gray stallion called Broken Arrow went off at forty-to-one, I had $6,000 on him to win. EZ nearly kissed me when it happened. The jinx was broken. He had a winner. I don't think he himself had any money on the horse, and I know he didn't know it was not his horse, because Ozzie Hirsch would not have told him: Ozzie's job was to bring in winners, not to prevent a champion being swapped for a nag. Probably Hirsch had something on the horse, but it could not have been much. The insiders were always watching to see when a trainer, directly or not, put money down on a horse—his mount or someone else's. When that happened everyone in the business eventually got word, the bucks piled on and the odds dropped hard. Allen Sloane was in a better position: not only could he lay money down through his organization in Los Angeles, but he was connected to other bookmakers around the country. Even a huge amount could be artfully placed, with a good part of it laid off on other horses to prop up the odds. God only knows how much he made. A million at least, this at a time when you could build a nice mansion in Beverly Hills for $20,000, and a 1939 Cadillac coupe could be had for $1,700. With the money I made—the IRS barely existed then—I could afford both: it was almost a quarter of a million bucks. I was set.

And scared. That morning I had been a Negro screenwriter running out of time on a six-week contract. I was behind in my rent at the Garden of Allah. My car needed a valve job. I hadn't bought a new suit in a year. Suddenly I was a player.

"You bet on my horse," EZ said to me. "Larry, you showed faith. You bet on EZ Shelupsky." The man was glowing. "That Ozzie Hirsch, I told you he was a pro. Horses, they're like the movie business—you got to believe in the impossible. Here is a nag that was a born follower, and now he's a leader. How much you make?"

"I should have bet more," I said. "I do believe in you, EZ."

"I should have believed in you, Larry. You got something in your brain that translates to success. A spark. A whole fire. I'm proud of you like you're my son. You know what?"

"What, EZ?"

"I'm going to make you a partner."

"A partner?"

"Half and half. We're going to make Jewish movies. I'm going to look over your treatment, and if it's got anything to it I'm going to take you in fifty-fifty."

"Fifty-fifty?"

"Straight up," he said. "Half the investment, half the profits. I got to go to the winner's circle now. They're decorating flowers on my horse. Forty to one. They didn't believe. But I believed. You believed. This photo I'm going to make sure is going to be on the front page of every paper in Los Angeles. EZ Shelupsky's Broken Arrow a winner, comes from nowhere and wins bigger than all the horses of producers of white movies combined. You like champagne? Go ahead, drown your happiness in it. Waiter!"

IX

That afternoon when I was to meet Fritz at the bungalow—I'd given him a key—I planned to say nothing about the win. Part of it was shame. Here was a guy making a hundred a week, practically starvation wages in this business, and I was holding onto a fortune. But mainly it was caution: In the back of my mind I was afraid he might hit me up for a loan. I knew he sent money to people in Berlin—at our first meeting he'd questioned me on the "political reliability" of Western Union—though he never talked about them. If Fritz were to ask for money I'd be embarrassed to turn him down. But I would have had to. As—if they'd known about my good fortune—I would have had to turn down a whole list of others who would have come knocking at my door, including my comrades in the Party. I'd never been good with money, but then again I'd never really had any. Now I did.

It took me less time to turn into a capitalist than to turn off Sunset Boulevard onto Havenhurst looking for a place to park. I knew I would find Fritzi sleeping on the sofa. Somehow I didn't feel like making him coffee. It wasn't that I was suddenly better than Fritz. It was that it could hardly matter: the writing team of Bellringer and von Blum had accomplished precious little. In a matter of days I had to turn in a treatment—not a script but merely a three-page outline—and even that was nowhere in sight. What was in sight I recognized immediately as I parked. I doubt there were two cars like it in Los Angeles County, maybe in the whole state.

"Hello, Larry," Allen Sloane said to me from the green leather sofa. "You do well at the track?"

"Not bad," I said.

"I was just talking to your writing partner here. Very educated gentleman."

Fritz stepped out of the kitchenette with a highball in his hand, a smile on his face, and a serious buzz on. Behind the thick round lenses his eyes were shiny as the bottoms of shot glasses. "You have such an interesting friend, Larry. We have much in common."

"*He's* a refugee," Sloane said. "They want to make *me* one. Doesn't get more in-common than that."

"*Hodie mihi, cras tibi*," Fritz said brightly, then helpfully translated—into German. "*Heute mir, morgen dir.*"

Just what I needed: he was really drunk. Any lingering hope that we might grind out a quick treatment went, as EZ might say, *foof*. Considering that I had joined the ranks of the rich only hours before, the threat of unemployment remained a potent presence. I was disappointed in myself, angry at Fritz, and afraid.

"Know what that means?" Sloane asked. "I bet you do. A Harvard man like you."

"Tell me."

"What's to me today," Sloane said, "tomorrow to you. Fritz taught me. What do you think of that?"

"*At's whay otay emay odaytay, omorrowtay otay ouyay*," Fritz said.

Hindi? Serbo-Croatian? "What?"

"Larry, this little guy, he speaks what, four, five languages—German, English, French, Spanish, Latin, what else, Fritz?"

"Good German."

"I said that one."

"But *good* German. The best." Fritz smiled broadly. "Better than Hitler. Better than Goering. Better than Goebbels, no question."

"There was another," Sloane said.

Fritz thought a moment, a drunk looking down into his treasure chest, unsure what it contained. "Greek?"

"*Ancient* Greek," Sloane said. "That, too."

"And . . ." Fritz said. "And . . ."

"Larry. The guy speaks *languages*. He's got a feel."

"Esperanto," Fritz said finally, having exhausted his search. "Es-per-an-to."

"I never even heard of that one," Sloane said. "The guy speaks languages nobody heard of."

Fritz stretched his thick little body out on the couch, his small feet like the dots in exclamation marks. Still smiling blissfully, he dozed off. Then, abruptly, his eyelids flew open behind the thick lenses. "*Esperantoway isway ethay anguagelay ofway opehay.*" His eyes closed again. He was out.

"You got that?"

"Fritzi and I are supposed to be working," I said. "We're on deadline."

"He'll be okay. Give him an hour. 'Esperanto is the language of hope.' Little guy picked up Pig Latin in *otway akesshay ofway away amb'slay ailtay.* What do you say to that? If we ever get into a war with Hitler this guy—guys like this—I want them on my side."

It was coming back to me, like roller skating or checkers. "Two shakes of a lamb's tail?"

"See that?" Sloane said. "What better proves I'm as much an American as anyone? You grew up with Pig Latin in New York, I grew up with it in Cleveland. Aside from this being very inconvenient, the feds trying to deport me, it happens not to be right. I mean, say it happened to someone else, I'd still think so. It's just wrong. I'm not a Russky or a Canuck. I'm a Yank."

"Probably a rich one, after today."

"Nah," Sloane said. "I was rich before. What's rich? You got some money in your pocket? In the bank? It's how you feel. I've known hobos feel richer than Rockefeller, and probably there are Rockefellers—minor, outlying ones maybe—feel poor next to the big ones. I guess you made out okay."

"Six grand to win."

Sloane whistled appreciatively.

"I had to borrow the money from all over. My parents. Imagine that. Twenty-nine years old and I had to borrow from my folks."

"You can certainly afford to pay them back."

"Oh yeah," I said. "With interest."

"Now all you got to do is pay me back."

Suddenly the room felt drafty, even cold. The windows were wide open. It was overcast outside, not looking like rain, but the sun was veiled behind a peculiar thick, blue fog. Though I didn't know it at the time, this was the beginning of the smog that would be associated with L.A. for decades, made worse when manufacturing and oil refining grew almost geometrically to satisfy the needs of a country at war. Things would change: women and Negroes would join the work force in factories, the movie business would gear up for war and then grow like crazy afterward until it bumped into television. All those new workers would be driving cars. Freeways would be built. Houses would sprout in endless patches of subdivision around the exit ramps, then supermarkets and churches and schools. More people, more cars, more smog. But for now, there was only an indefinite chill as the sun was obscured by an unfamiliar blanket of blue. I slid shut the patio doors and the two casements at the side of the room. Now I could see the haze inside. Both my guests had been smoking heavily. Blue outside, blue within. "Payback time?"

"*Oneway andhay ashesway ethay otherway.* One hand washes the other."

"Allen, what could I possibly do for you? I'm just a screenwriter." I paused. It didn't seem like enough. Surely I could do worse. "A Negro, faggot, Commie, screenwriting hack."

"Who went to Harvard."

"They can put it on my tombstone. It's not really much good otherwise."

"Depends."

"On?"

"You went to law school."

"For a year."

"Harvard Law School."

"It doesn't count unless you graduate, Allen. Then you've got to pass the bar. Without following through it was just an idea. My parents' really. They thought I should be a credit to my race. In the end they got a son with credits in race movies. I wouldn't have made much of a lawyer. Law school put me to sleep."

"But you went to law school with *people*."

Where was he headed? "That's the way it usually goes, Allen."

"I looked you up."

"I'm sorry?"

"Harvard, class of '33. Harvard Law, class of '36."

"Except I quit in '34."

"You said." Sloane reached into the inside breast pocket of his suit jacket—single-breasted, the coming style, precisely what I planned to go out and buy, his a soft, loosely woven tan. The hat beside him was dark brown, with a thin tan band. On his feet were artfully made white-and-brown oxfords. For a straight white man, he had style. "Let me give you some names. You tell me if they ring a bell."

He started reading from a typed sheet in a curiously thin voice, maybe an octave higher than normal, as though he had rehearsed it and needed to succeed. I had seen actors do this at auditions when there was more than a role at stake. Immediately I recognized the names. He must have gotten hold of the list of the class of '36. To each name he appended a title, or a description. It was easy to see how he was such a good handicapper of horses. He knew more about my former classmates than I did, maybe more than they did. Two were clerks to federal judges, about a dozen worked for the Department of Justice directly, one was with the FBI, one with Immigration, three were in the State Department, a dozen or so were in state government, including two in California. "The rest are in private practice or business," he said. "One died—tuberculosis, that's a killer. Larry, you Harvard Law guys, you are at the top of your profession. There isn't a sweet spot you aren't in."

"Allen, I'm not a Harvard Law guy."

"For my purposes, you are."

"What purposes?"

He folded the paper slowly, slipped it back into his breast pocket and at the same time with his right hand pulled the gold cigarette case out, effortlessly extracted a Viceroy, and lit it with the gold lighter that appeared in his left. Magic. He took a long drag, sucking hard through the crude filter. That's the way they made them, then. In the gay community—we didn't call it that, then—we sniggered that we knew what it meant when a fellow sucked hard on a Viceroy. Of course, straights smoked them too. "Larry, maybe I don't look like it, but I am a desperate man. I'm going to be kicked out of my own country. If that happens, and I don't have Vitamin P, I'm going to end up in some jungle-bunny country, no offense, where the currency is coconuts. I got someone I love who wants to be with me, but it's going to be hard for both of us in Bora Bora."

"Allen, you lost me at Vitamin P."

"Vitamin P. Protection. I need some help from people in a position. I'm well connected in certain quarters, but in others, like federal judges, you might say I'm a stranger. When I heard you are a Harvard man and went to Harvard Law School to boot, I concluded you are my ticket."

"For the last time, Allen, I'm not anyone's ticket to anything, much less Vitamin P. I'm just a colored queer."

"Does it hurt you to try?"

"You want me to try?"

"That's all I'm asking. I did for you."

"You did, and I'm grateful. But I don't know what I'm trying for."

"You're trying to help me out. I'm a friend. A friend tries to help a friend."

I found myself sighing. Allen Sloane was right. I

didn't know what it was I was trying, but the least I could do was try.

Fritz slept on.

X

The next day, September 3rd, Britain, France, Australia and New Zealand declared war on Germany. Call me callow, but I recall the date because Fritz showed up at the Garden of Allah with a sheaf of papers he pulled out of his battered German briefcase.

"It is the land of liberty, so I took it," he said, and sat down heavily on the green leather sofa. He lit a Chesterfield. "Would you like to read?"

"Read?"

He handed me a folder. Neatly typed on a square, red-bordered, yellow sticker on the front page was this:

HOOFBEATS OF LIBERTY
an original film script by
Laurence Bellringer and Fritz von Blum

Someone had crossed out "film" and replaced it with the word "movie" in a delicate and formal hand. I flipped to the last page, one-twelve. "Who wrote this?"

"We did," the little man said.

"We? I didn't."

"Certainly you did. We wrote it together. You and I. We sat, we talked, we worked, we plotted. We created."

"We created?"

"I typed," he said.

"This is a whole script, Fritz. I don't know how good it is, but it is a script."

"Larry, it is a marvelous script," he said. "Full of history, romance, heroism. It resonates, if that is the correct word. *Acta est fabula.*"

"The story has been completed?"

"Perfect, my dear Larry. And they say all Negroes can do is play jazz music and tap-dance."

"Apparently we can write entire scripts without putting one word on paper."

"*Adde parvum parvo manus acervus erit.*"

"Add a little . . ."

"Add little to little and eventually there will be a big pile."

There remained the question: A big pile of what? I sat down in the easy chair opposite the green leather couch, upon which Fritz was already stretching out, and turned to the first page. By the time I got to the second Fritz was asleep. When I reached the end I went to make a pot of coffee. "I've never read anything like this," I said, while the little man held a steaming cup in his hand and looked down into it as though it contained more secrets, more structure, more dialogue, more tension, more laughter, more tears, more . . . life. "Fritzi, how did you do it?"

He sipped from the coffee. "*In magnis voluisse sat est.*"

"In big . . ."

"In great things," he said, "will is enough."

XI

Looking back, 1939 was a hell of a year. A loaf of bread cost eight cents; Kate Smith, America's sweetheart, was on the radio endlessly belting out *God Bless America*, which was written by an immigrant Jew who called himself Irving Berlin; Pan American started regular flights across the Atlantic; DDT was invented and so were nylon stockings; *Gone With the Wind* won the Oscar for best picture; the Spanish Civil War ended; the Germans marched into Czechoslovakia and conquered Poland; London was bombed by the Luftwaffe; the World's Fair opened in New York; and EZ Shelupsky burned down his own studio.

Maybe not. In Hollywood cynicism comes easy. But the timing was just too convenient. For weeks after, jokes flew around town about Jewish arson—"Hey, Izzy, you should get flood insurance also." "Flood insurance? How do you make a flood?"—and were reprised when EZ announced he was not going to rebuild but sell to a real-estate developer. The jokes were more good-natured than anything else, because it was no secret that race movies did not have much of a future, and the only people who would miss them were the colored actors who would not find work in mainstream pictures. Aside from maids and chauffeurs, there were not a lot of roles for darkies: When Hattie McDaniel won an Oscar that year for her role in *Gone With The Wind*, it seemed not so much to refute this sad fact as to emphasize it. But change was also in the air.

In New York, a fellow named Barney Josephson opened a nightclub called Café Society that publicly welcomed racially mixed clientele; by 1940, there were three such clubs in Los Angeles—of course, the queer bars had been integrated for years. Some of this loosening up was an indirect reaction to the race hatred that came out of Germany like a stench—*Confessions of a Nazi Spy* was a huge hit at the box office. The crushing end of the Spanish Civil War as well as Stalin's pact with Hitler hadn't left many causes for the American left: Ending racial prejudice became a rallying cry.

For a long time it had been clear the country was not exactly hot to join the British and French in "their" war—icons like Charles Lindbergh and Henry Ford spoke out strongly against U.S. involvement, and they were listened to. And there was popular sentiment that went further than isolationism: on Washington's birthday that year, the German-American Bund brought over 20.000 American Nazis to a rally at Madison Square Garden in New York where Roosevelt was booed and Hitler cheered. Despite this, when Germany invaded Poland on September 1st and the other Western democracies entered the war two days later, there was no question where the U.S. was headed. Where I was headed was a meeting with EZ Shelupsky to determine the fate of a script.

With his office destroyed and his studio in ruins, the producer had me come to his home in the San Ysidro Canyon, next-door to Pickfair, which Douglas Fairbanks had bought for Mary Pickford, and where she still lived with her second husband, Buddy Rogers. You couldn't see Pickfair from EZ's property. Too much of EZ's property was in the way. It looked like the Alhambra, but with less restraint—and many more palm trees. The pool alone was as big as a lagoon and feverishly decked-out with boulders, ferns, flowers, parrots and macaws—neither the rocks nor the plants nor the tropical birds any more real than a backlot set.

"Alive birds," EZ told me from the chaise where he was smoking a six-inch cigar behind sunglasses so dark they seemed black. "They shit all over the pool, and in the morning they wake you up like Polish roosters. When it comes to nature, we got people in Hollywood can give you nature by the yard and even better than the original. This is some script, Larry."

"Just something Fritz and I tossed off," I said.

"When you told me New York, New Amsterdam, whichever, I figured dark, dark houses, dark furniture, big Pilgrim hats, but it turns out the story of the Jews in America is cowboys and Indians and horses. I swear, Larry, you got so many ponies in this script they might get credits. I'm not going to obfuscate you. This is one hell of a script."

"It was important to get it right."

"You want coffee?" He picked up what looked like a telephone receiver. "Adelphia, bring out a pot of coffee and some little sandwiches." An electric squawk emanated from the loudspeaker in reply, as though someone had shouted back, overloading it. "She'll never learn," EZ said. "Been with us for years. Faithful as a dog, but not good with modern devices." As quickly he switched to the subject at hand. "You like working with him?"

"Him?"

"The refugee."

"A treasure," I said. "One of the most educated people I ever met."

"Yeah, I know. Speaks Greek."

I considered. Maybe Fritz spoke Greek to EZ Shelupsky and Latin to me. No, I thought. "And Latin."

"That, too."

"Really helpful, EZ. I'm glad you paired us."

He puffed on his cigar, the smoke dissipating into the California air as though it had never been. "I had to.

Some Jewish group comes to me, 'Do something about these poor Jews in Germany. Sponsor one for a visa.' First I said, 'Why? I'm not a Jew—I'm an American.' So this fella says, 'You're a Jew, Mr. Shelupsky. Everyone knows that.' I tell him, 'My friend, in America, what you want to be, you are.' So he says, 'Let's make a scientific experiment. We'll call up three people, you pick the names, and I'll ask them, 'What's EZ Shelupsky?' You know what, Bellringer? All three said, 'He's a Jew.' Then I thought, If I hadn't come here as a kid, I'd still be in Poland today, and you know who just took over Poland. So I said why not? A couple months later the refugee actually shows up and he wants a job. Not just a hand-out. Got a wife and two kids in Germany. I say to him, 'Dr. von Blum, why are you here alone without the wife and kids?' Daughters, I think, little ones. And he says, 'You only sponsored *me*.' Poor guy, he is so worried about them he starts to bawl, right here where you're sitting. And now with the war especially. But they'll be OK. That Hitler is nothing but a big bag of wind."

"He never mentioned he was married," I said.

"Yeah, well, we all got our cross to bear. He got a Star of David."

Whether this was meant to be funny, I didn't know, and still don't. But just the thought of Fritz having a wife and kids gave me a creepy feeling. Suddenly I wanted to get away, jump into my newly repaired Ford and drive. But instead a kind of fierce independence welled up in me. "Are we going to make the movie or not?" I asked.

"What movie?"

"*Hoofbeats of Liberty*."

"Yeah, sure. It happens I don't have a studio at the moment, but that doesn't matter, because the last thing I need to make a Jewish movie is colored actors. And this is a big movie. We're talking location, we're talking stars, we're talking livestock, we're talking major promotion. It's going to cost three quarters of a million bucks. Easy. Maybe more. But it'll pay. Jews are a big topic today. If it wasn't for that Hitler, probably not. But every day we get our promotion right out of the headlines. I been talking to some people. How would you feel about Doug Fairbanks as the Jewish priest?"

"Douglas Fairbanks?"

"He was my neighbor, right over there behind the jungle. Then him and Pickford broke up. Her, she's a little tra-la-la. But Dougie is solid like a rock. Very distinguished."

"I was thinking more like John Garfield. Douglas Fairbanks doesn't look particularly Jewish."

"Exactly," EZ said. "You don't want Jews in movies to look Jewish, otherwise people who aren't won't identify. If I can't close with Doug, what do you think about Gary Cooper? I could probably borrow him from Universal. Barney Balaban owes me a favor. I mean, it would cost, not just for Cooper but to Universal, but they'd distribute. That's a plus. Gary Cooper, that would be one dynamite Jew."

"I don't know, EZ."

"Of course you don't. You're new at this end. But I'll show you the ropes. Larry, you'll be my pertejay."

"Your . . . ?"

"Pertejay. I'll take you under my wings. You wanted to be a partner?"

"Yes, of course."

"Then you got it."

"I do?"

"Sure," EZ said, waving his cigar. "How much you want to put in?"

"Put in?"

"Put in. Larry, we're talking heavy investment, heavy profits. I'll put in half a mil. You?"

"EZ, I don't have that kind of money."

"You made a quarter mil on one bet, Larry. Don't tell me you spent that already."

"How do you know how much I made?"

"What do you think, I'm stupid? I'm on the board of Hollywood Park. If I don't know who's betting what, who does—the ponies? Also, it was *my* horse." He smiled. "Allegedly."

I waited. "Allegedly?"

"Do me a favor and give me a little credit, Larry. You think I don't know one gray beast from another? I got close to fifty animals in my colors, and I know every one of them like I fucked them an hour ago. If I didn't I wouldn't be a horse owner, I'd be a would-be. I appear like a would-be to you? Look around." He motioned with the cigar so expansively that its aroma could have smelled up the horizon. "Wrong I have been. You make a lot of bets—on women, horses, pictures, people, okay, some you lose. But stupid? Stupid I'm not. You want to be a partner with EZ Shelupsky, Larry, you got to put in cash. You know what I want from you to make this Jew movie? Two hundred thou. You drive that crappy Ford to keep people off the scent, but I know you got it."

Just then EZ's maid came up with the coffee, and poured it while looking directly at me.

"Adelphia," he said. "You ever meet Mr. Laurence Bellringer? He's going to be an important man in this town. Hell, maybe he's going to be the most important colored man in the whole movie business."

Adelphia looked at me with undisguised loathing. It was bad enough being a maid, the look said, but worse to have to serve another Negro and pretend he was something else.

"Nu, Larry?" EZ said. "You wanted it? Here it is on a plate. Try these little sandwiches, smoked whitefish. Flown in from Chicago. Really delicious."

XII

EZ Shelupsky never held it against me for not putting my money into a Jewish movie, and I suspect this is because for him the simplest way to judge whether something was worthwhile was whether other people would risk it. Besides, it turned out EZ was already involved with other things.

The script Fritz wrote, which cost $3,600 in writing fees to both of us, EZ sold to Universal for $20,000, which after the war dumped it on Paramount for $12,500. Paramount, which was releasing a movie a week, actually made it, with Dan Duryea as the priest, but by this time the priest was no longer a secret Jew, and there was no continuing story of the first Jews arriving in Nieuw Amsterdam or the priest's grandson who grows up to supply horses to the Revolutionary Army. I saw it in London, where it played in Piccadilly on a double bill with a Danny Kaye musical, after which it disappeared completely. They did get in the business about the priest teaching the Apaches how to ride and breed horses, but it was hardly Fritz's script. Did Fritz ever see it? I would have asked him if I'd had the chance.

Shortly after our collaboration, Fritz was invited to Washington to work for a part of the government that would become the Office of Strategic Services—after the war, it was renamed the CIA—and when war broke out he joined Army Intelligence where eventually he was on the prosecution team during the Nuremberg Trials. After the war I heard he resumed his work in Washington, or elsewhere. I know he never set foot again in Hollywood. His wife and children never made it out of Europe.

The war changed everything.

Nora Bright left EZ Shelupsky after his studio burned down, but that was to be expected. What wasn't was that EZ went to the World's Fair in New York and discovered something called television. Determined not to make the same mistake he had made when talkies came in, he threw himself into the new medium, investing heavily in local stations in California and then setting up a production company to create variety shows, including one in 1956 that starred Nat King Cole—the first show hosted by a Negro with white guest artists. Southern stations turned their backs, but the show was a success with viewers, and EZ eventually produced other shows with black performers. Whether it was his background in race movies or simply because he got along with colored entertainers, he became one of the major players in early television—if there was a Negro in it, EZ had a piece. On and off, I worked for him as a writer and then as a producer into the '60s, when he slowed down to spend more time with his beloved ponies. His horses won the Belmont and the Preakness, but he never had a mount in the winner's circle at the Kentucky Derby. He was, however, an honorary Kentucky Colonel, which reflected his rank in the U.S. Army Signal Corps during the war. "I had nothing better to do," he liked to say, "because Hollywood Park was closed until V-J Day." He made dozens of films for the army, including all the training films for Negro soldiers, which often featured his old colored stars from Racetrack. A 4F, I was exempt from the draft, and as a civilian wrote most of those scripts. After the war EZ liked to be addressed as "colonel," and as he grew older became one of those Hollywood legends whose life story was told and retold as though he had lived with the fossilized saber-tooth tigers in the La Brea Tar Pits off Wilshire Boulevard.

Whenever I saw him he kidded me about the Jewish movie, or asked with a straight face whether I was ready to settle down with a wife and start a family and give up being a queer, but only that once did he mention the switched horse. I avoided bringing it up, not least because I knew that he knew that I knew Allen Sloane had been behind it.

After the war, Sloane remained in London where he did quite well. He had a Thames-view suite at the Savoy, a Bentley and chauffeur—"I don't like driving on the wrong side"—and a flourishing business directing what would become England's largest bookmaking operation.

"Funny how things work out," he told me at his hotel, where the waiter at the American Bar opened a bottle of house champagne for us without a word being spoken. "Here it's legal." He placed his large hand on mine, the violet of his cuff peaking out from a bespoke sleeve. As ever, he was dressed beautifully, now in the British fashion, his suit a symphony of thin gray-and-purple stripes on black, his tie a pale silver. As before, he smoked with an unaffected elegance that I envied. "And it's all because of you."

"One hand washes the other," I said. "You bet on me."

"And you came through."

It hadn't been much. I made some calls, eventually reaching an old roommate at Harvard who worked for the Department of Justice. He asked me to tell him everything

I knew about Allen Sloane, and then he made some calls. Within a week, Sloane was on his way to England on a British *laissez-passer*. The British were short of ships and planes and tanks and ammunition, but what they were most short of was pilots.

"I get here, they say, 'How are you on night flights? Basic instruments, that sort of thing?' I say, 'I still own a plane in California. I been flying nights ten years.' Right then and there they make me an instructor in the RAF training program at Usworth—that's way the hell up near Newcastle—with the rank of captain. They had to give me a rank because otherwise in the way things go here nobody would pay attention, and then one day they say, 'Would you mind terribly much taking command of a squadron of Hurricanes since you've been teaching how to fly them?' And I said, 'Why not?' Good thing, too, because it was just in time for what they call the Battle of Britain. When that was over we started escorting bombers, Lancasters and Blenheims, over Germany, and I was Major Allen Sloane, RAF—how's about that?—and everyone was saluting me, and I became what they call an ace. And then the war is over and they pin some fruit salad on me and tell me thank you very much, now you can go home."

He poured some champagne for me, picked up his glass and clinked mine. "Chin-chin," he said, his eyes narrowing in the semi-dark of the hotel bar. He sighed. "So I said, 'Gentlemen, I'm embarrassed to say I don't have a home. I'm not an American citizen. I'm a man without a country.'" He smiled. "So somebody calls somebody, just like you did, and then somebody invites me to the Home Office, and documents are prepared, and in just the time it takes to place a bet on a horse I become a British subject, swearing loyalty to the king, and a few people I know from the RAF come by and say, 'Allen, old chum, is there anything you'd like to do now you've no Jerries to shoot down?' So I told them what my old profession was, and they said, 'Jolly good, we'll back you. Least we can do and all that.' And they did, and here I am."

There were two questions on my mind. Sloane was beaming. I went for the first. "EZ's lady, the one you were fucking better than him."

He smiled. "Left me when I joined the RAF."

"She wasn't much of a lady then," I said.

"You're right about that." He turned, facing me directly. "I was a little hard on you, back in L.A."

"Hard on me?"

"Calling you a queer."

"Well, it's accurate," I said. "At least you didn't call me a nigger."

"That would have been just as bad," he said. "Considering."

"Considering?"

"You really don't know? EZ never said?"

"I never mentioned you."

Sloane stood, took off his bespoke jacket, folded it neatly on the maroon leather banquette so that its bright magenta lining shone in the dim room, then sat back down again. A tiny ridge of moisture appeared on his brow. "That was no lady," he said. "That was . . . "

The waiter appeared, poured out more champagne, then disappeared.

"That was . . . ?"

"A guy."

It took a moment. I picked up my champagne—really good champagne, but I would have been happy for kerosene—and drained the glass. "You're telling me . . . "

"It was just something that happened. I never knew I was like that, like you, and it's not something that happens a lot now. I mean, I like ladies, but in that particular case I happened to fall in love with a . . . guy. A very feminine guy. A colored guy, actually. Not very colored, much lighter than you. Almost lighter than me. When we met I thought he was a woman. What did I know? From the outside you couldn't tell."

"This *guy* was EZ's lady? You're telling me that EZ is queer?"

"I don't know," Sloane said. "He was married to a lez, and he never had kids, but it could be he was in my situation. Suddenly he met someone—this was a beautiful person, physically, and kind of mysterious—and maybe the same thing happened to him that happened to me. Hey, I didn't know I was going to be an RAF officer, or an Englishman—it just happened. Things happen." He smiled. "Well, Larry, you made it happen, and for that I'll always be grateful."

"But I didn't make you . . . "

"A queer?"

"A queer."

"But I'm not, not really. Hey, sometimes it happens, but it's more like I'm everything. To tell you the truth, remember that horse we switched?"

"Of course."

"I would've fucked *him*, too. That was one beautiful horse. A champion. You had to love that horse. I loved him the first minute I saw him, and he was wild, not even saddle-broke. I'm not even embarrassed to say this. I knew he could run, but it was more than that. I loved him. So what does that make me, queer for animals? Okay, then I'm queer for animals. I also like good clothes and nice cars. I guess I'm a mental case, right?"

"No more than any of us," I said, thinking of EZ Shelupsky with a colored queer, in love with a colored queer, and then of Allen Sloane stealing him away. Well, I thought, *there's* a story that will never be a movie. "And the horse?"

"What about him?"

"What happened to the horse?"

"He stayed with EZ. I mean, you can't swap a horse back."

"So you got EZ's . . . lady, and he got . . . "

"My horse," Sloane said. "I never looked at it like that. If you do, maybe EZ got the better deal. All I got was a broken heart. I should have kept the horse."

"Then you wouldn't have ended up here."

"Yeah, I would've ended up in Panama. I guess we both came out of it okay, EZ Shelupsky and me. But I'll tell you, that was one hell of a horse. A guy in New Mexico calls me, says he has a horse—a guy I'd been doing business with. Frankly this is not the first time I switched a horse. Of course, with lip-tattooing you can't do it anymore, not here either, not even in Ireland, though it still happens in France. So I go out to look and . . . this is some horse. Turns out to be one of those wild horses the Indians had, but in looks, in everything horse, this was like a throwback to the Spanish horses, a pure small thoroughbred. Nobody could tell it wasn't a thoroughbred. It must have been descended from those horses the Spanish brought over. What they call the Izquierda Line."

I turned away. Someone was playing a piano in the far corner, and I tried to concentrate on listening to the notes. It was *Over the Rainbow*, a jazzed up version that would not have been recognizable when the movie came out in 1939, but now seemed right. It was as if I were hearing it for the first time, and hearing it I was back for a moment when Allen and Fritz and EZ had all crowded together into my young life. When I looked back, Allen was pulling on his jacket.

"Really good to see you again, Larry," he said. "Anything I can ever do for you, you let me know. You know what Fritz used to say?"

"No, what?"

"*Tempora mutantur et nos mutamur in illis.*"

"The times change . . ."

"The times *are* changed, and we are changed in them. One hell of a smart guy, Fritz."

"Yes," I said. "You hear from him?"

"Fritz? Nah, nobody hears from him. He's not a regular person. I don't have to tell you. You know what else he said?"

"Tell me."

"*Quidquid latine dictum sit, altum videtur.*"

"Anything said in Latin . . ."

Sloane waved to the waiter, then took my hand in his, squeezing it in farewell. "Anything said in Latin," he said, "sounds profound." He winked, and—like the confident clarity of my own youthful promise—was gone.